Evening

The sight of Sally walking toward him
stopped his remembering. He wanted to get
up and go into the cabin, but couldn't because she had seen him. So he remained on
the step, enduring the strange discomfort
that overcame him whenever he saw her.
At least, working with the carpenter, he
didn't have to be around her all day anymore, afraid to speak to her and more
afraid when she spoke to him.

"Evening, Ras."

"E-e-evening, Sally," he managed to say
before looking away quickly. Her voice was
soft, reminding him of the warm breezes of
early spring. Sometimes he wanted to curl
up and go to sleep with her voice wrapped
around him. There were times when he
wanted to touch her black skin with the
tips of his fingers as if he were stroking
the high, deep night sky. But Sally wouldn't
want him to do something like that. He
knew that.

Vicki Grandison

Also from Point

by Julius Lester

To Be a Slave

THIS STRANGE NEW FEELING

Julius Lester

SCHOLASTIC INC.

New York Toronto London Auckland Sydney

ISBN 0-590-32924-3

Copyright © 1981 by Julius Lester. All rights reserved. Published by Scholastic Inc., 730 Broadway, New York, NY 10003, by arrangement with E. P. Dutton, Inc.

12 11 10 9 8 7 6 5 4 3 2 1   12   5 6 7 8 9/8 0/9

Printed in the U.S.A.   01

For

Elena Nilad

and

David Julius

THIS STRANGE NEW FEELING

This Strange
New Feeling

One

1

Jakes Brown didn't know what to think that July morning when he saw the young black man waiting for him by the toolshed. He was big, with muscles like ropes bulging from his torn and dirty cotton shirt. He was Jakes's height, five feet nine inches, and weighed one hundred eighty pounds at least. Yet his shoulders were rounded and his back had a slight stoop to it, as if he were an old man. In the torn pants that barely covered his knees and the sleeveless shirt, he looked like a stuffed and weathered scarecrow. But he couldn't have been more than twenty years old.

"My name's Jakes Brown," the young white man introduced himself, holding out his hand and smiling.

"Yes, sir," the black man responded in a monotone, staring at the ground.

Jakes felt foolish with his hand extended, and after a moment let it drop. "What do I call you?" he asked, determined to be friendly.

"Ras."

"Ras what?"

"Ras, sir," he said, still staring at the ground.

Jakes wondered if he had been given the dumbest slave on the plantation for a helper. Ras? What kind of name was that? A man had to have two names, or at least one that made sense. Ras!

Jakes took a key from his pocket and unlocked the shed. Well, what did it matter to him? All he wanted to do was finish the job, collect his pay, and get back home to Maine. "You know where the tobacco shed is, Ras?"

"Yes, sir."

"Well, you're going to help me build another one right beside it."

"Yes, sir."

"Call me Jakes. Everybody does."

"Yes, sir."

"Didn't you understand me?" Jakes flared, irritated with the dull response.

"Yes, sir."

"Aw, forget it!" he exploded. "Bring them tools and sawhorses over to the shed. When you finish that, you can start carrying that lumber stacked behind the toolshed."

"Yes, sir."

Jakes walked away angrily, sorry now that he had decided to come South for the summer. But he'd heard that work was plentiful dur-

4

ing the summer and that the wages were good. He was young and strong, and had thought it would be fun to do something different. It would give him some good stories to tell through the long, cold winter. But nobody would believe there was a creature as dumb as Ras. And after you said he was dumb, there was nothing more to tell.

All morning Ras carried tools and lumber, understanding now why Master Lindsay had had them clear new ground last fall and plant more tobacco this spring than they ever had.

Ras's shoulders still ached thinking about the chilly mornings, fog lying over the ground like scraps of cotton, as he and Uncle Isaac cleared the woods on the other side of the field. He smiled, remembering how he had made that double-headed axe ring against the trees until they trembled, swayed, and then fell as slowly as a large hawk alighting on a branch. Ras supposed he and Uncle Isaac had cleared fifteen acres by themselves.

His shoulders ached, too, remembering how he and the other slaves had worked through the winter to prepare the newly cleared ground for planting. He hated that most — burning the cut trees and how he smelled of smoke and ashes for weeks afterward. Then he and the other slaves spread the ashes over the field, raking and pounding the ashes into the soil. Now he was going to help build the new barn where the tobacco would hang until it was cured.

Ras wondered sometimes if he would have rather been a mule. Coming in from the fields at evening, he would stop at the corral and look at the mules inside. He supposed there were some differences between him and them. But the differences seemed to be to the mules' advantage. They had four legs to his two. When it rained or was chilly, they stayed in the barn. They had as much to eat as they wanted. Ras couldn't remember Master Lindsay ever selling a mule, either.

He didn't know how old he was when Master Lindsay sold his mother. Aunt Jessie told him how he had cried and cried when he came in from the field to find his mother gone.

"You was a little fella then," Aunt Jessie said. "It was your first summer in the fields. You had to pick the worms off the tobacco leaves."

Ras remembered. He remembered, too, that Aunt Jessie and Uncle Isaac had taken him to their cabin and spread straw in a corner for him to sleep on. Time passed, and one day he cried because he couldn't remember what his mother looked like. More time passed, and one day he tried to remember her voice and it was gone, too, and Aunt Jessie had died and couldn't put her arms around him and tell him, "It's all right, child," though she didn't know what was wrong. Finally the day came when nothing remained except a name — Mother — and he didn't know what that was.

A mule didn't need to remember its mother. A mule didn't know it had ever had one. Once Ras imagined himself asking one of the mules to exchange places with him. He knew that the mule hadn't answered, but he swore he heard a voice say, "A mule has got more sense than to want to be a slave."

2

In the evenings Ras sat on the steps of the cabin he shared with Uncle Isaac in the slave quarters. The twenty cabins were lined in two rows facing each other, a dusty clearing stretching between. They were built with cheap lumber or logs and had no windows. But the cracks between the boards and logs allowed in light, and in the winter the cold. Each cabin was a small, dark room with a fireplace for cooking. Those who knew how built chairs and tables. They were few. No one had beds; they slept on boards and covered themselves with the thin blankets Master Lindsay gave each slave at Christmas. A blanket never lasted the winter.

Ras watched the slaves as they returned from the fields, talking quietly as they went wearily to their cabins. He had already eaten his supper of cornmeal cakes and a strip of bacon. If he had worked in the fields that day, however, he might have gone to sleep without troubling to build a fire, grind the corn into meal, mix it with water, and put the dough on the hot coals to cook.

The sight of Sally walking toward him stopped his remembering. He wanted to get up and go into the cabin, but couldn't because she had seen him. So he remained on the step, enduring the strange discomfort that overcame him whenever he saw her. At least, working with the carpenter, he didn't have to be around her all day anymore, afraid to speak to her and more afraid when she spoke to him.

"Evening, Ras."

"E-e-evening, Sally," he managed to say before looking away quickly. Her voice was soft, reminding him of the warm breezes of early spring. Sometimes he wanted to curl up and go to sleep with her voice wrapped around him. There were times when he wanted to touch her black skin with the tips of his fingers as if he were stroking the high, deep night sky. But Sally wouldn't want him to do something like that. He knew that.

"Been missing you in the field, Ras."

"Master put me to working with the white carpenter."

"Ain't you the lucky one!" she exclaimed.

He shrugged. "It's all the same."

"I reckon," she agreed.

The door of the cabin opened and a tall dark man, his face covered by a full white beard, stepped out. "Thought I heard you, Sally," he said in a loud, strong voice.

"Evening, Uncle Isaac." The girl smiled. "How're you this evening?"

"Doing all right for an old man." He chuckled, sitting down beside Ras.

"Don't say that too loud," she responded. "Master Lindsay will put you back out in the field."

Uncle Isaac chuckled. "Don't I know it? He came down here last week talking about he could use another hand in the field. Told him I was too old to be working in that hot sun all day. Told him that he put me in the field, I might not be in any shape to haul his tobacco into town for the auction come fall." He chuckled again. "Well, he backed off then. He knows that there ain't nobody in the state of Maryland who can grade and bale tobacco as good as me. He'd be lost without me. He told me to rest up and take it easy." Uncle Isaac laughed loudly.

Uncle Isaac's laugh was one that enjoyed laughing. When others heard it, they found themselves smiling and laughing to themselves, though they didn't know what had been said. It didn't matter. When Uncle Isaac laughed, it was as if you were being tickled on the bottoms of your feet by invisible fingers.

"Uncle Isaac," Sally began, when she had managed to stop her laughter, "if you were younger, I'd marry you."

The old man snorted. "Huh! What age got to do with it? Sit down here, girl! Let an old man show you what these young ones can't." And he laughed even louder.

Ras laughed with them. He wished he could

think of funny things to say as easily as Uncle Isaac, wished that his laugh made other people happy just to hear it. But after he said "Good evening," he never knew what was supposed to come next.

Maybe he was afraid to tell Sally that when he saw her, he felt like a tiny bird hopping from limb to limb in a tree on an April day. But he didn't want to come in from the field one day and feel like a tree chopped down by a double-headed axe when he learned that she had been sold away. So he said "Good evening" and fell into a silence as deep and still as a well.

3

Scarcely a week passed before Ras knew the names of all the tools, could saw as straight as any man Jakes had known, and could put a nail through a two-by-four so quick, you had to look twice to be sure he hadn't used a sledge. If Ras had known how to read, write, and do figures, Jakes could've made him into a first-rate carpenter. But something gave Jakes the feeling that Ras could build the next tobacco barn without anybody's help.

Some people were like that. Learned by doing, but couldn't read their name if it was written in letters ten feet high. Nonetheless Jakes was enjoying teaching Ras what to do and the various ways of doing it. To Jakes's surprise, he never had to explain anything to Ras more than once, and sometimes Ras seemed to know before Jakes finished talking.

Jakes liked to talk, and though Ras never responded, Jakes talked all day, remembering all the good times he had had up in Calais, Maine (which he pronounced Callus). And on one of those afternoons, while talking about how beautiful and peaceful it was in Calais, and how he wished Ras could go there, he had an idea.

He thought about it for several days, and the more he thought, the more he liked it. Now that would sure give him something to talk about when he got back. When he got to be an old man, he could tell his grandchildren about how he had helped a pitiful colored boy escape from slavery. Even better would be to take Ras back when he went. That way Jakes could teach him to read and write, show him how to walk into a store and buy a suit of clothes and how to hold his head up and look a man in the eye.

"You ever think about being free?" Jakes asked Ras eagerly the next morning.

"No, sir."

"What?" he exclaimed, shocked. That wasn't what he had expected Ras to say. "What's wrong with you people? You mean to tell me that you're happy spending your life as a slave?"

"Yes, sir" came the dull reply.

Jakes started to tell Ras just how dumb he was but stopped, wondering suddenly if Ras was dumb. After all, what would he have said to such a question if he'd been Ras and Ras him? Would he have trusted a white man who just opened his mouth and started gabbing about being free? He knew he wouldn't have.

Jakes decided that he would just talk. He was sure Ras would drink in every word like a mule drinking water after swallowing the dust of the field all day. "Bet you didn't know that the next state north of here is a free state."

Ras didn't respond, but took another nail from his teeth and began hammering.

"This here is Maryland," Jakes continued, raising his voice above the sound of the hammer. "You go north from here and in four, five days of steady walking, you're in Pennsylvania. That's a free state. Not a slave in it. Lot of free colored people there. Some of them dress better than any white man, too."

Jakes glanced at Ras, but couldn't tell if he was listening. But he continued, telling Ras about Philadelphia and New York and Boston. "Too many people in those cities for me. I like a small place, like Calais. Little bitty place, right on the border between the United States and Canada. Canada is a whole separate country. Fact is, Calais is the last town in these United States. You leave Calais, walk a couple of miles, and you're in another country. Done it many a day."

Jakes talked about the winters when it snowed from October to May. "Sometimes the snow on the ground is taller than a man."

Every day Jakes thought of something else

to tell Ras. "I don't know what I like better — getting up early in the morning, taking my rifle, and going out to hunt deer, or going out to sit on a boulder and fishing in a fast-moving stream. And let me tell you, as far as I'm concerned there is nothing in this world better than the sweet soft flesh of a fish for good eating. Just thinking about it makes me want to get off this barn and walk all the way back to Calais right now."

When summer ended and the barn was finished, Jakes could only conclude that his words had bounced off Ras's woolly head and disappeared in the air, because not once had Jakes detected even a flicker of interest. He never asked any questions, never smiled, never nodded or shook his head. Just took a nail from the side of his mouth and hammered it through a piece of lumber. If Jakes had wasted his breath talking to a chicken all summer, at least the chicken would've clucked every now and then.

Well, he didn't care. Why should he? Ras didn't have any worries. He had a place to live, food to eat. Not like a white man, who had to get out and earn the money to put a roof over his head and food in his belly.

No, Ras wasn't dumb. Why should he want to be free like Jakes, free to starve, free to sleep in the woods, which he'd done many a night, and would do again probably. While Ras, dumb Ras, would have a house and a full belly.

Ras reached his hand gingerly into the hot ashes and jerked out the cornmeal cake. He let it lie on the floor to cool for a minute before breaking off a piece to put in his mouth. He chewed slowly, frowning as he tasted the mushy, uncooked center. He considered returning the cornmeal cake to the embers, but was afraid he would let it overcook this time. So he broke off another piece and let it slide down his throat.

"Uncle Isaac?" he called softly through the dark interior of the cabin.

The old man lay on his plank at the other side of the room, and when Ras heard a mumbled "What is it, son?" he knew that Uncle Isaac had fallen asleep. But he had to know.

"Uncle Isaac? Have you ever eaten fish?"

"Fish?" Uncle Isaac asked sharply, fully awake now. "What're you asking me something like that for?"

"You ever eaten any?" Ras persisted.

Uncle Isaac rose slowly and moved over to the fireplace, where he sat down on the floor next to Ras. "When I was slaving on the Trent plantation in Virginia. There was a stream run right through the plantation and Master let us catch as many fish as we wanted."

"Did?" Ras asked, amazed.

"I dream about that sometime, you know.

I sure do. Master Trent let his slaves have their own garden, too."

"Did?" Ras repeated, unable to comprehend a slave master being so kind.

"Son, me and Jessie would grow collard greens, spinach, carrots, and all like that. I hated it when Master Trent died and his son sold me and Jessie over here. Master Lindsay is one of the stingiest masters I've ever seen." The old man shook his head in disbelieving dismay. "But that's not what you asked me about. What you want to know about fish for?"

Ras looked at Uncle Isaac as if he had never seen him before. Just think! He lived with someone who had actually eaten fish! "What did it taste like, Uncle Isaac?" Ras asked, his voice brimming with reverence.

Isaac's eyes were flooded suddenly with tears. "Don't want to talk about it," he said gruffly. "Don't do no good to think about them days. It makes tomorrow harder when I think about yesterday."

"I bet it was good," Ras said, his eyes shining.

Uncle Isaac stood up abruptly, wiping his eyes vigorously. "Always did make my eyes tear when I sat too close to the fire," he mumbled. "Believe I'll go sit out in the cool awhile."

It was late, and as Uncle Isaac sat on the porch step, he could not hear a sound from the cabins lining the quarters. There weren't even the dull yellow points of candlelight to be seen between the cracks of the cabins.

He wiped at his eyes again, but that did not stop the tears or the trembling in his stomach as he remembered the look in Ras's eyes. He'd had that look once. But there'd been Jessie to think about. And live in slavery with her was better than being a free man without her. So time passed, the look faded from his eyes, and the laugh grew. Laughing was a way of being free too.

He supposed he'd been lucky. He and Jessie had never been sold away from each other. But the tears spilled from his eyes to trickle down his face, and behind the tears his eyes acquired a gleam that shone with the hardness of the sun on the blade of a hoe. And he wondered, as he had so many times, if it would not have been better if they had at least tried to run away.

He knew that the three children Jessie birthed didn't die because they were sickly. The way she cried told him the truth. Even after she was too old to birth babies, he would be awakened in the night by the sound of her crying in her sleep.

She had smothered them babies with her own hands. He never saw one of them alive. Each time when the midwife called him in, the babies was dead. Looked big and healthy to him. Boys, each one of them. But they didn't grow up to be slaves.

He never said anything to Jessie about it and she never said anything to him. Sometimes, though, he would look at her while they were working in the field and her face would be so wet with tears, she looked like someone had thrown a gourd of water on her.

The night Ras came to the quarters and found his mother had been sold away, Uncle Isaac didn't ask Jessie and she didn't say a word to him. She went to the boy and Uncle Isaac went to find straw for him to sleep on. Jessie stopped crying in her sleep. He was glad that the last five years of her life she didn't have to cry anymore.

Uncle Isaac wiped his face. Ras. He didn't have a Jessie to change the gleam into a laugh. He was a good boy, but the crying and laughing seemed caught inside him, like a rabbit in a trap that would never be set free.

Uncle Isaac chuckled. Fish. Then he laughed aloud and his deep voice seemed to rumble forth from some deep hole behind the stars. Fish! That was as good a reason as any for wanting to be free.

Two

1

Thomas McMahon was a fat, bald white man who sweated profusely, summer and winter. Uncle Isaac had never seen him when he wasn't mopping his round, slick head with a big red handkerchief and breathing noisily, as if he had just finished running five miles.

Now, that would have been a sight!

Yet of all the white men Uncle Isaac knew, Thomas McMahon was the one. It was more than a feeling Uncle Isaac had about him, though the feeling was important. McMahon was the only white man in that part of Maryland who didn't own slaves. Uncle Isaac guessed that he still had about a hundred acres left from all he'd sold over the years, and he could've been a rich man if he had owned slaves. Yet except for the few acres he planted in tobacco, vegetables, and hay, his land was overgrown with trees and underbrush. And God was perhaps the only one who remembered the last time his house had been painted. The barn was beginning to lean as if there were a constant wind blowing against it. He was a strange man, but he was the one.

Almost absentmindedly Isaac ran the tip of his forefinger over his thumbnail. It was as hard and thick as the blade of a plow, but it was the mind behind the nail that made the difference. It took a man like Uncle Isaac, who knew tobacco better than he knew himself, to look at a tobacco plant and know precisely where to cut the top with his thumbnail. That was what made the tobacco grow large, sometimes seven feet high with leaves six feet long.

Uncle Isaac had heard white men offer Master Lindsay $2,000 for him. That was a lot of money for an old slave who did no heavy work. But Master Lindsay wouldn't think of selling him. Isaac was allowed to hire himself out, though, to the other planters. However, he had to give half of what he earned to Master Lindsay. Uncle Isaac supposed if Jessie was still alive, he would've spent the money and bought chairs, a table, clothes, and food. But caring about such things died when she died. He kept the money in a sack that he hid behind loose bricks in the fireplace.

As Uncle Isaac made his way through the woods that Sunday afternoon, he didn't think what he would do if Mr. McMahon turned him down. There wasn't another white he'd dare present such an idea to, not if he cared about his life. But when he remembered all the years he had used his thick thumbnail on Mr. McMahon's tobacco, and how he always invited Isaac to sit in the shade of the porch and drink a big glass of lemonade and then talk all afternoon, Isaac knew. Thomas McMahon was the one.

When McMahon looked up from the shade of the porch where he sat in his rocking chair and saw Isaac walk out of the woods, he wondered how old Isaac was. He looked as old and eternal as God, with the big white beard like clouds around his black face. But he walked as easily as any young man, and certainly more nimbly than McMahon had ever walked. Isaac had to be eighty if he was a day. Any slave who lived that long was not only strong but wise in the ways of a wicked and hard world. And that made Thomas wonder why Isaac was coming to see him on a Sunday afternoon.

"Afternoon, Mr. McMahon," Isaac said easily as he crossed the dusty yard the chickens had picked clean of grass.

"Howdy, Isaac," McMahon returned in his high-pitched nasal voice, which reminded Isaac of a weak train whistle.

Uncle Isaac stopped at the edge of the porch and the two men stared at each other for a moment. Thomas mopped his head with the big red handkerchief and looked into the dark eyes imbedded in the black face. He shifted uncomfortably, knowing it was insolent for a black to stare him in the eye like that. For an instant McMahon wished he was the kind of white man who would've knocked Isaac down for looking anywhere else except at the ground.

"It's strange to see you over here, Isaac," he said coolly. "You took care of my tobacco a while back, as I recall."

"Yes, sir," Isaac returned evenly.

McMahon couldn't withstand Isaac's stare any longer, and he wiped his face with the big handkerchief to escape from those eyes. "What can I do for you?"

"Nothing for me, sir." Isaac smiled.

McMahon wanted to be annoyed. Why didn't Isaac just say what he wanted? But that wasn't his way. He made you come to him, and despite himself Thomas McMahon knew he would.

"Mind if I set down here on the steps, sir, and rest these old bones?"

"Sit if you want to," Thomas returned gruffly.

Isaac sat down, his back to the fat man in the rocking chair. "Your tobacco turned out right well."

"Can't complain."

"Right well," Isaac repeated. "You plant about four acres, don't you, sir?"

"You know that as well as I do."

Isaac ignored the ragged edge of annoyance in McMahon's voice. He nodded slowly, and then turned and stared directly into the white man's eyes. "I always thought it was strange that a man with as much land as you own wouldn't plant thirty, forty acres of tobacco." His voice was no longer casual, and his statement sounded like a challenge and rebuke.

"I do all right," McMahon managed to say, startled by the abrupt change in the conversation. "What business is it of yours?"

Isaac smiled and turned back to stare over the field where the tobacco was growing. "It must've hurt you mighty bad when you had to sell off another twenty acres last year."

McMahon's face turned even redder than its normal strawberry color. "What's it to you?"

"When you sold that land, I thought you was going to buy you some slaves for sure this time, and plant the hundred acres you got left in tobacco so you could earn some money to do you some good."

"You got some slaves you want to sell,

Isaac?" McMahon asked sarcastically.

Isaac laughed. "Now wouldn't that be something? A black man with slaves to sell." He laughed loudly, and just when McMahon began his tittering wheezy laugh, Isaac turned his whole body around and said firmly, "I got a slave I want to free."

McMahon felt his jaw drop, and the sweat slid off his head and down his face. "Are you crazy?" he gasped, wiping his face and neck nervously. "I could have you whipped to within an inch of your life if I told Lindsay what you just said."

"But you wouldn't," Uncle Isaac said with quiet confidence. "Not if I know anything about people."

"What — what do you mean?" Thomas McMahon asked, unable to hide his curiosity, believing in spite of himself that this old black man was about to answer for him the riddle his life had been.

"It took me a while to understand it, Mr. McMahon," Isaac said conversationally. "I'd think about you with almost two hundred acres of rich land, good land. And I've watched you sell off half of it over the years. And it didn't make sense. I'd say to myself, 'Now here's a white man who could be one of the richest slave owners in the state of Maryland. But he scarcely lives better than poor white trash.' So I asked myself, 'Why would a man who could be rich deprive himself?'"

"Well, you know so much. What's the answer?" McMahon asked, with obvious forced anger.

Isaac smiled softly. "Because he can't bring himself to do what other men do to make themselves rich."

"Maybe," Thomas allowed after a long pause. "Maybe," he repeated, adding hurriedly, "But that don't mean I'm a fool! I don't know what you have schemed up, but let me tell you this. I don't plan on going to jail for helping a slave get free. And that's final!"

Isaac erupted into a big laugh. "Jail? Who's talking about jail, Mr. McMahon? I'm talking about New York."

Thomas stared at Isaac for a moment, and when he understood, a smile spread slowly across his chubby red face. He wiped his head and chuckled. "Isaac, if you weren't so old and decrepit, I'd take a horsewhip to you for putting ideas in the head of an old, fat white man who's never done much with his life." He laughed. "You think it'll work?"

"I know it will, sir. I know it will."

The two men laughed until tears streamed down their faces, and then they laughed some more.

2

It was the last Sunday in September when Thomas McMahon gave a low whistle and the two horses jerked into motion, pulling the wagon filled with bales of tobacco. The sun was showing orange over the horizon as Thomas began his annual trip to New York to sell his tobacco.

In past years he had dreaded this trip, necessitated by the dislike the other planters and poor whites had for a man who had freed the slaves he had inherited from his father. If he had known then how long they would refuse to do business with him, he might have kept the slaves. Forty years had passed, but they hadn't forgotten.

As a young man of twenty-two he'd only wanted to do the right thing. But what had been right for those blacks had been a disaster for his own life. He supposed he could've sold the plantation and moved North, but McMahons were known for being stubborn. So he'd stayed and gotten so fat he could scarcely fit into a rocking chair. It was as if he had been punishing himself for being different. Two hundred eighty pounds of blubber sitting on the porch and watching the weeds grow.

Yet an old black man, as ancient as the Big Dipper and as wise as the earth that knew how to turn a tiny seed into a seven-foot-high tobacco plant, had seen something worthwhile in him.

When he got back he would ask Isaac how he had managed to see beneath all the fat and know that Thomas McMahon hated slavery. Thomas had always believed that he'd freed his father's slaves because he was too lazy to run a plantation. But he knew now that he hadn't wanted to remember how his father had made him watch slaves whipped, or the light-skinned children who were his half-brothers and -sisters, though no one said so, or the day his father had taken him to slave auctions to teach him to judge "nigger flesh." Thomas hadn't wanted to remember, so he'd convinced himself that he was too lazy and set the thirty slaves free.

This Sunday morning it was thirty-one. Thomas chuckled as he thought about the tobacco tied in bales in the wagon behind him. Even if he told someone, they wouldn't believe that at the bottom of the wagon, wrapped inside a bale of cured tobacco leaves, was a young black man whom Isaac called Ras.

3

Ras stared through the window of his room in the white house on Center Street in Calais, Maine, marveling yet again at the snow piled high outside. Two months had passed since the night he had unrolled himself from the tobacco leaves outside the warehouse in New York City, where Thomas McMahon took his tobacco to sell. Only two months. It seemed like a life lived by someone else.

If anyone from that life had seen him now, they would not have recognized the erect man in the dark suit with the cravat at his throat. And if they had asked his name. he would've answered proudly, "Ras McMahon." His landlady called him Mr. McMahon, and only occasionally did he forget that she was speaking to him. Once, while walking along the street, he happened to see a smiling reflection in a store window and walked half a block before realizing that it was him. That's what freedom looked like, he concluded.

The days passed with a leisureliness that was almost mysterious. It was a curious feeling to sleep as long and as often as he wanted, to eat fish until his stomach ached. With the money Uncle Isaac had given him Ras would not have to work until spring, at least. Calais was a lumbering town, and he knew he could swing an axe as good as any man. Being free now, he thought he could fell a tree with a single swing. Free! It was such a tiny word for something so big.

It was early on a cold morning at the end of November when the door of his room was flung open suddenly. Ras awoke immediately and sat up in bed to stare at a gun in the hand of Master Lindsay.

"There you are, you scoundrel!" Lindsay exclaimed.

"I told you! I told you!" came a voice from the hallway, a voice vaguely familiar to Ras. But before he could remember where he had heard it, Jakes Brown walked hurriedly into the room.

"That's him!" Jakes said excitedly, his eyes going nervously from the still and silent Ras to the room's pink wallpaper and back.

"I saw him walking down the street one day, dressed as fancy as a white man. Now, where's that reward money you mentioned when I wrote you?"

Lindsay reached in his coat pocket and handed a pouch to Jakes. "Twenty-five silver pieces, like I promised."

Jakes grinned greedily, opening the pouch and thrusting his fingers inside. "Thanks, Ras. I might've starved to death this winter without you." He laughed nervously and hurried from the room and out the door.

"Well, Ras. What you got to say for yourself?"

Ras's eyes widened as he looked at his master, and suddenly tears rolled down his face. "Oh, Master! Master!" he sobbed. "Master Charles! You don't know how glad I am to see you. You don't know!"

Lindsay was startled. "What're you talking about?" he asked warily.

"Oh, Master! Running away was the biggest fool thing this here black boy ever did. It's so cold up here, Master! And the white people up here, they don't treat a black man good like you do. Master, I'm so glad you come for me! So glad, Master!"

Ras sprang from the bed and ran across the room, where he threw his arms around Master Lindsay's knees and hugged him. "Oh, Master! I just didn't know what to do without you telling me. I didn't know when to get up and when to go to sleep."

Master Lindsay laughed with delight.

The day Ras returned to the plantation with Master Lindsay, the slave owner called all the slaves together. "You know Ras. He ran away up North. I want you to listen to what he has to say."

Ras stood on the porch of the big house and looked out over the crowd of slaves gathered in the yard beneath him, and at Sally directly in front with tears in her eyes.

Ras forced his mouth into a big grin. "It sure is good to see you all. You don't know how much I missed you. I didn't know how good living here was until I got up North. I didn't know how much I needed a good master like Master Lindsay to tell me what to do until I went up North. I'm so happy to be back here with Master, who'll put a roof over my head, and food in my belly, and tell me what to do. And if I need anything, all I got to do is ask Master, and if he thinks I need it, then he'll give it to me." Ras looked at his master. "Thank you, Master. Thank you for giving this ignorant slave one more chance. Thank you, Master."

Master Lindsay smiled. "That's a good boy, Ras. Now, I hope you all heard him," he declared to the slaves shivering in the chill of a cloudy autumn afternoon. "Ras is a smart boy and I hope you all will be as smart. Now, to celebrate Ras being back, I'm giving you all the rest of the day off."

Lindsay was surprised that his announcement was not greeted with cheers and grins.

The slaves moved away quickly. Some glanced over their shoulders at Ras as if he were a dead man they wished had stayed buried.

Ras followed slowly, and when he reached the slave quarters, everyone had gone into their cabins. The closed doors looked like walls to him. But as he went up the steps to the cabin he had shared with Uncle Isaac, he heard a door open. Turning, he saw Sally running across the clearing toward him.

He smiled. "It's good to see you, Sally."

She slapped him so hard, he tasted blood in his mouth. "Listen good, Ras!" she said angrily. "Listen good, because this is the last time you'll hear my voice or that of any other slave around here. I just hope you feel good after walking over a dead man's grave the way you did up there at the big house."

"What're you talking about?" he asked, holding his cheek and swallowing a thin trickle of blood.

"Don't you know?" she exclaimed loudly. "Know what?"

She laughed harshly. "Well, this is going to be a pleasure. That Monday morning after it was clear you'd run away, Master Lindsay come down here to the quarter and asked Uncle Isaac where you were. Uncle Isaac say he don't know. Master Lindsay didn't believe him. He tied Uncle Isaac from that big oak back of the big house, tied him upside down by his ankles, and then whipped the black off him. Blood was dropping off him so fast, it sound like rain. You hear me? But every time Master Lindsay ask him where you were, Uncle Isaac don't say a word. And when he died, he still hadn't said one word." Tears of anger and sorrow poured down Sally's face. "So I hope you proud of yourself. You better be, 'cause you gon' be one lonely man around here."

She spun away, but Ras grabbed her arm and pulled her back to him. She raised her free arm to strike him, and Ras grabbed that arm and held her tightly.

"Now you listen!" he said in a low and ominous voice. "I'm real sorry about Uncle Isaac. Real sorry. But I ain't got no time for tears now. If you believed all you heard me say up at the big house, then you a bigger fool than Master Lindsay."

"What?" Sally exclaimed softly.

"What do you think he would've done to me if I hadn't said all that? He would've sent me to join Uncle Isaac in the boneyard! Don't you have any sense, woman?" he said fiercely, flinging her away from him.

Sally looked at him, unable to believe that this was Ras standing before her, his body bursting with strength. Freedom must be more wonderful than she had ever dreamed.

"Ras?" she offered timidly. "I — I'm sorry. I should've known better."

He nodded and Sally returned to his side to let her hand rest softly in his. He said, "I knew about Uncle Isaac. Master told me on the trip back from the North. I didn't cry then. I'm not going to cry now." Then, looking deep into Sally's eyes, he said firmly, "Ain't none of us gon' cry anymore, Sally."

4

Charles Lindsay was furious when he discovered five slaves missing a month after Ras returned. Ras was furious, too, and when all the slaves had been called to the big house, he gave an even better speech than the first one.

"Them slaves what run away was just ungrateful! Master done taken care of them when they was sick, given them food, a place to live, and work to do. I met white folks up North that would be happy to have what we got down here."

The slaves nodded in agreement, and that night laughed themselves to sleep.

Lindsay and other planters searched for a week for the missing slaves. In the course of one day's futile searching a planter mentioned that Thomas McMahon had gone to New York to sell more of his tobacco. "I wish he would stay there," another planter commented bitterly, and thought no more of it.

Through the mild winter and into early spring slaves continued disappearing, and Ras sympathized with Master Lindsay. "They just hardheaded, Master. I feel sorry for them."

"Speaking of being sorry," Lindsay began, "I been meaning to tell you something. You remember Jakes Brown, don't you?"

Ras would never forget him.

"I got a letter recently from someone I met up there in Maine, and he told me that Brown killed himself. Shot himself in the head. I feel more sorry for him than I do for those dumb slaves who think they're going to be better off in the North."

The next month, five more slaves disappeared one night. Master Lindsay was afraid now. That many slaves couldn't disappear without help from someone. The other planters agreed, and one rainy night they met at Lindsay's to talk the matter over.

As they sat around the long oak table in the dining room after dinner, they scarcely noticed Amos pouring the snifters of brandy and passing around a box of cigars. Since the death of Uncle Isaac, the gray-haired old man was the oldest slave on the plantation. He was butler in the big house before Charles Lindsay was born, and was as much a part of the place now as the tobacco in the fields. That was how the planters regarded him, forgetting that tobacco didn't have ears.

The slave owners smoked cigars, sipped brandy, and admitted that if someone was running slaves off the Lindsay place, it was only a matter of time before slaves started disappearing from their plantations. After more cigars and more brandy, they agreed that they had to hire armed guards to patrol their plantations every night from sundown to sunup. It would be expensive, but losing slaves was disastrous.

"Sometimes I wonder if Tom McMahon isn't the smartest one of us all," a planter commented.

"What do you mean?" another asked sharply.

"Well, sometimes I wonder, who is the real slave? Us or them? We're as much enslaved to them, if not more. How many of you go to sleep at night worrying if you're going to wake up in the morning and find your barns burned down, or the legs of your mules busted."

"You got a point there," someone else put in.

"Sometimes I wonder if that's what Tom figured out forty years ago, and that's why he let them prime slaves go free."

Another man chuckled. "Well, I don't know about that, but I do know that ol' Tom must have himself a lady friend up there in New York."

"How so? Tom McMahon with a lady friend?" somebody laughed.

"I know it don't make sense, him with a lady, but seems like every month here recently, he's been going up to New York. All his tobacco was sold last fall. So what else would take him to New York if not some lady he met up there?"

"Just goes to prove what we've known all along. A Yankee woman will love anything."

The men started to laugh, but the laughter

was stopped abruptly by the sound of Charles Lindsay's fist hitting the table so hard that cigars perched on the edges of ashtrays fell off.

"We're a bunch of fools!" Lindsay exploded. "A bunch of fools!"

There was a stunned silence as the realization settled through the room that Mc-Mahon had been running the slaves.

"Well, if it wasn't raining cats and dogs, I'd say let's go to his place now and burn everything we can set fire to," someone said finally.

"There's always tomorrow night," Lindsay said with finality.

On that the meeting ended, and the planters dispersed quickly into the stormy night.

It was late before Amos was able to sneak away from the big house and go down to the slave quarters, where he told Ras what he had overheard.

"Thank you, Amos," Ras said when the old man finished.

"I'm not doing it for you," the old man said haughtily. "I know what you been doing. Master Lindsay don't know about your part in it, yet."

"You going to tell him?" Ras asked menacingly.

"If it was just you, I would've told him a long time ago."

"Then why?"

"This is for Isaac. Master Lindsay shouldn't have done that. I've known him since he was a little baby that wasn't able to turn from his back to his belly. I never thought he'd grow up to do something like he did to Isaac."

"Thank you anyway, Amos. And if you don't hurry back to the 'big house,' Master Lindsay might do something to you."

Amos smiled at that. "Oh, no. Not me. I practically raised him."

While Amos was passing his information to Ras, Charles Lindsay lay awake in his big feather bed, thinking about Thomas McMahon's trips to New York and wondering if McMahon had made a trip around the time Ras ran away. He wondered, too, why no slaves had run away while Ras was gone, and so many since he had returned.

He would have gone to sleep with these thoughts if he had not heard a door closing on the ground floor of the house. He got out of bed quickly, slipping into his bathrobe. Lighting the candle on the nightstand beside his bed, he took his pistol from beneath the pillow and went rapidly and quietly down the stairs. There, in the kitchen, water dripping off him, stood Amos.

"I didn't mean to make so much noise as to wake you, Master," Amos said with a smile.

"Where you been?" Lindsay asked roughly.

Amos took off his wet coat. "I thought I heard some noise coming from the quarter.

I thought some of them trifling slaves might be trying to make off in the rain."

Lindsay grabbed Amos by the arm and put the pistol to his head. "Amos, I know you better than you think. And I know you wouldn't go out in the rain if it was Judgment Day. Now what were you doing down in the quarter? You weren't telling Ras about the meeting tonight, were you?"

The old butler was surprised that he was not afraid. "Are you going to do me like you did Isaac?" he asked calmly.

Lindsay released Amos and, without a word, returned to his room, where he dressed warmly against the chilly rain outside. Maybe he had lost his touch. Maybe he was getting too old to handle slaves. Come spring he would sell them all, including Amos. Move to New Orleans or Savannah and go into business.

Shoving his pistol in his pocket, Charles Lindsay went out into the night.

5

Though there was no light as yet, Ras and Sally could see the dim outline of the foot-bridge ahead.

"How far you think we come?" Sally whispered.

"Don't know," Ras lied, knowing that the heavy rain had made traveling difficult. They had not come very far at all.

"Are we going to stop and rest soon?"

"As soon as we cross that bridge, we'll find a place to hide during the day and get some rest."

"I hope it's a sunny place. I'm so wet and chilly, I'm afraid I'll catch my death."

Ras had awakened Sally minutes after Amos left, and they had started immediately. He would've preferred to wait until the next night and get an earlier start. But if Master Lindsay had figured out about Mr. McMahon, it wouldn't take him long to realize who had been taking the slaves to Mr. McMahon.

"Let's go," Ras whispered.

They stepped out of the woods, crossed the clearing, and started across the bridge. Beneath them, running through the deep gorge, they heard the thunder-roar of the river swollen by the torrential rain of the night.

They were midway across when Charles Lindsay stepped out of the woods on the other side and blocked that end of the bridge.

"Oh, Ras!" Sally screamed.

"Run, Sally! Run!" Ras yelled, pushing her away as he ran toward Lindsay, his fists clenched.

Lindsay had just pulled the pistol from his coat when Ras reached him and grabbed his wrist. The two men struggled briefly, but Ras's bare feet could not grip the rain-wet boards of the bridge, and he slipped, pulling Lindsay down on top of him.

Lindsay struck Ras in the face and a tiny string of blood dribbled from a corner of

Ras's mouth. The white man grabbed Ras's throat with one hand and pointed the pistol at his forehead with the other. Ras grabbed the wrist of the gun hand and pushed it up. Lindsay squeezed Ras's throat tighter and tighter. Tears came to Ras's eyes and he began to gag for air. His grip on the wrist of the gun hand began slipping, and he could feel Lindsay's arm coming lower and lower. The breath in his body became thinner and thinner, and though he knew the sun was rising, everything was becoming black.

Suddenly there was the sound of a gunshot. The hand at Ras's throat relaxed and Charles Lindsay fell on top of him.

"Ras! Ras! Ras!"

Ras opened his eyes slowly, gasping for air. Through his tears he saw Sally standing above him, Master Lindsay's pistol dangling from her hand.

"Ras! You all right?"

He managed to nod. He pushed Lindsay's body off him and got up slowly. Sally dropped the pistol and flung herself into his arms. "I was so afraid, Ras," she sobbed. "I saw him pointing that gun at your head, and I didn't know what to do, Ras. I didn't know what to do."

Ras managed a wheezy chuckle. "It doesn't seem that way to me."

She shook her head. "I guess I snatched the gun out of his hand. I don't know. I just couldn't let him kill you. I just couldn't let him kill you."

The rain had stopped, and from the rapidly clearing sky the rays of a soft dawn were warming them. Ras lifted the body of his dead master and dropped it over the bridge, watching as it fell slowly through space and into the river so far below.

They stared into the river for a long while, watching it swirl and crash down the gorge. Sally rested her head against Ras's chest. Her body trembled with cold and fear and he pressed her to him.

"Let's go," he said finally. "We need to sleep."

"Not yet, Ras," she said quietly. "Not just yet. I — feel so strange."

He looked at her and was surprised to see a smile on her lips. He knew that smile and the tremulous flutterings in the stomach that went with this strange new feeling of freedom.

"Let's go," he repeated quietly, hugging her even tighter. "You'll have the rest of your life to get used to that feeling."

She shook her head. "It's too good to get used to, Ras. I want being free to feel like this always."

And so did he.

Where the
Sun Lives

1

When the overseer rings the bell to wake the
field hands, it is not daybreak yet. Sometimes,
if Mistress Phillips has had a bad night, I am
awake and hear the bell. I am jealous of the
field hands, because they have slept through
the night. Their work has a beginning and an
end. Sometimes mine has pauses.

Last night Mistress Phillips's fever came
back. I sleep on the floor at the foot of her
bed. When I was a little girl, I slept lying
across her feet to keep them warm, a thin
blanket over me. She turned from her back to
her stomach to her side throughout the night,
and I would get kicked.

I'm bigger and older now. Mammy Sukey
said she thinks I'm eighteen. In the winter I
sleep in the bed with Mistress Phillips to help
her stay warm. Before Master moved to the
other bedroom, I slept in the bed with both of
them. In the summer I sleep on the floor.
Sometimes I wonder what it would be like to
sleep without being waked, to sleep through

the night and through the day and through the night again.

Mistress Phillips coughs and I hold the basin under her chin as she gags. She sinks back into the bed, hatred in her eyes as she stares at me. That don't mean nothing. She hates me because she's dying and I'm not. I guess she's angry, because she's always had me to do whatever she wanted. Now she wants me to die for her and I can't.

"Master be here with the doctor soon," I tell her.

She just stare at me. She know the doctor can't do no good. He might take a little blood, but that don't seem to help. I guess don't nothing help when you dying except to die and be done with it.

I get up from the side of the bed.

"Where you going, Maria?" comes her hoarse voice.

"Just to raise the window, Mistress. Let some of the cool morning air in for you."

I cross the room and raise the shade of the window that looks out over the yard and down to the slave quarter. I see a man on a horse, a black man riding slow and quiet, like he doesn't want to wake the morning too rudely. He rides up through the slave quarter and past the stand of pine trees. There's a big heavy-looking sack tied across the horn of his saddle. I can't see his face in the light of false dawn, but he must be handsome. I know, because you can tell a lot about a person from the way they walk or sit on a horse.

He sits on that horse like it is part of him. He's past the overseer's shack and is headed toward the stable. If I didn't know better, I would swear he knew where the sun lives.

"Maria!"

"Yes'm," I respond, raising the window quickly and hurrying back to the bed. "I'm right here."

"What were you looking at out that window?"

"Nothing. Just looking. That's all."

"When I get well, I'll give you twenty lashes for staring out that window when you're supposed to be looking after me."

"Yes'm," I mumble.

That's one beating I won't have to worry about. Everybody know she ain't going to lay that rawhide whip on nobody ever again. She know it, too. It's just hard for her to believe it.

She closes her eyes and I hear the rooster begin crowing down in the chicken house. I wait. Way off in the distance, over on the Bradley plantation, a rooster crows. It's like that every morning. This rooster over here crows. Then, a minute later, the Bradley rooster crows. They'll be crowing at each other for the next hour now. I wonder what they be saying to each other? Wonder if this rooster telling Bradley's rooster about Mistress Phillips? Or maybe this rooster is telling about the black man on the horse.

I place my hand on Mistress's forehead. She knocks it away.

"I'm not dead yet," she growls, pushing at me weakly. "You think I'm going to die, don't you? That would make you happy, wouldn't it?"

"No'm, Mistress. No'm, it wouldn't."

Her eyes have a wild, crazy sparkle in them as she stares at me. I stare back, trying to put as much life in my eyes as I can. I want her to see all the life that's in me, all the life that she won't be able to take from me.

She closes her eyes.

"You not going to die, Mistress." She knows I'm lying, but I don't think it's a sin to lie to a dying woman. Especially one whose life wasn't nothing but one long day of suffering. Mammy Sukey said Mistress was one of the prettiest girls in Virginia. Mammy remember when she was born right here in this room, in this very bed.

I remember the first time I was brought up from the quarter to be her gal. I looked at her yellow hair and it made me think of buttercups and sitting by Miller's Creek with my dusty feet in the water. I was seven then. Mistress treated me like I was her little girl. She played little games with me, and at night would tell me stories. After she lost her first baby in the fifth month, she told me that it was all right, that I was her baby.

It was after she lost the third baby that she whipped me for the first time. I was in the kitchen that morning putting her breakfast on the big round silver tray to bring upstairs.

I turned around and she was standing in the doorway, the whip in her hand.

She told me to come outside. Then she told me to take my dress off. I was shamed to stand there in the yard as naked as when I come in the world. Mammy Sukey was pleading with Mistress, begging her to say what I had done wrong, and she would be sure I wouldn't do it again.

Mistress Phillips say that I hadn't done nothing wrong, just that it was time I learned that I was a slave. I ain't never felt nothing in my life as bad as the first time the whip cut my flesh. It was like somebody had taken a stick out of the fire and held it to me. I fell down in the dust and I don't remember nothing else. Mammy Sukey say that Master Byron had to come out of the house and jerk the whip out of her hand.

Next thing I remember was waking up and I was lying in Mistress's bed. She was putting cool salve on my back and my chest and tears were streaming out of her eyes. Mistress was saying how sorry she was and asking me to forgive her.

Soon as I was well, she didn't act like she was sorry anymore. After a while I could tell when she was going to get the whip. It was something about the way she would wake up in the morning, a look in her face like her eyes had died during the night. I don't know which I hated more — the whippings or her taking care of me afterward.

Now, sitting here on the side of the bed, watching her die, none of that seems to matter much. All that pretty buttercup-color hair is gray now. Her skin used to be as smooth as peach fuzz, and her cheeks were as red as fresh-picked raspberries. Now she looks like an old lady and her face is the color of old sour milk. Mammy Sukey said Mistress Phillips will be thirty in August. That's one birthday she'll have in the boneyard.

I hear the carriage coming up the road. "Master and the doctor coming, Mistress."

Her eyelids flutter but do not open. She probably doesn't care. Mammy Sukey said that Mistress never did want Master to be a lawyer and go into politics. She wanted him to stay on the plantation and run everything. She had been running the plantation since she was a girl of sixteen and her momma and poppa died when their carriage overturned near Cousin's Bluff. When Mistress married Master, she thought he would run everything then, and she could be a lady and give big parties. Least, that's what Mammy Sukey say.

The carriage stops in front of the house, and in a minute I hear the front door open and the sound of boots hurrying across the floor and up the stairs.

When Master walks in, he smiles at me. Doctor Carson don't look at me but goes straight to the bed. Master comes around to my side of the bed and puts his hand lightly on my shoulder. I look up into his face. His black, curly hair needs a comb through it and his eyes are red from driving all the way to Richmond and back. But he looks so young and she looks so old. I wonder if that's because he could never take the whip to any of the slaves. Mammy say that's why he decided to go into politics. He just didn't have the stomach for doing us like Mistress did.

I remember the argument they had just last month, right before Mistress took to bed for the last time. It was the day Mistress went down to the stable to get Baby, her favorite horse. I was standing behind her, just inside the stable door. Mammy Sukey's boy, Jim, takes care of all the horses, keeps them combed and pretty-looking, makes sure they get just the right amount of oats, and exercises them every day. With six horses to take care of, plus the mules from the field, Jim don't get much more sleep than I do.

When Mistress walked in the barn, Jim wasn't there. She called him, but he didn't come. I got scared. I don't know how I knew, but Jim had gone back to the quarter to take a nap. Mistress told me to go to the quarter to see if he was there.

He was asleep. When I woke him and he saw me, he knew he was in trouble. There's some things us slaves don't have to say out loud. We just know a lot of times what the right thing to do is.

I went back and told Mistress that he wasn't there. She said I was lying. I told her to see for herself. She went and Jim wasn't there.

That night Master and Mistress had the worst argument I ever heard. He accused her of making all the best slaves run off, told her that Jim was the best man in all Virginia when it came to caring for horses, that he was irreplaceable. She told Master that he didn't have no say in running the plantation, that he spent most of his time in Richmond drinking brandy and smoking cigars and she would do as she pleased with her slaves.

Wasn't nothing Master could say to that, or so I thought. He don't own none of us. We wish he did. All the slaves are hers, but he told her that if he ever heard of her making another slave run off and if she ever laid the whip on me again, he would kill her.

I heard that with my own ears. Mammy heard it and she was way out back in the kitchen. They were yelling so loud I wouldn't be surprised if folks in Richmond didn't hear. I know our old rooster had plenty to tell that morning.

When Master told Mistress he would kill her, she just fainted dead away. Me and Master carried her up to her bed and she hasn't set foot on the floor since. Maybe she going to die just to make Master feel bad. But as I leave the room to see if Mammy has breakfast ready yet for Master and the doctor, I think Master will probably look even younger once Mistress is in the ground.

When I walk out the back door, the sun is up. The roosters always stop crowing once the sun is all the way out. It's almost like they think their crowing is what makes the sun rise, and once it's up, then it can get across the sky on its own.

I cross the few feet from the house to the building behind, which is the kitchen. I notice the thin trail of smoke rising through the chimney, which means Mammy has the fire going and is probably kneading the dough to make biscuits.

When I enter the kitchen, a man is sitting at the table, drinking a glass of water. It is him. I can tell by the easy way he sits in the chair, his legs stretched out like snakes sunning on a rock down by the creek. His skin is brown and smooth like acorns. His face is serious. I could make him smile.

He sees me and I feel shamed in my thin dress that is so short he can see my knees. I don't want him to see me with my hair sticking out all over my head like porcupine quills. But I walk past the table, looking as if he's not even there. I lift my chin up a little, like I wouldn't stoop to speak to him if he was the last man in the world. I don't know why I act just the opposite of how I feel.

"How is she?" Mammy asks, her long thin fingers digging into the mound of dough and squeezing it quickly.

"About the same," I say, going over to the bucket in the corner and taking a sip of water from the gourd dipper.

"Was you up again last night?"

"Yes'm. Mistress's fever was pretty bad."

Mammy Sukey is as thin as a limb that broke off a tree in a storm. Master say she's as old as the wind. She not too much bigger than a spring breeze, but she work as hard as anybody around here. Wouldn't nothing be the same without Mammy.

She has put the kettle of water on the stove, knowing I like a good strong cup of coffee in the morning. I take a can off the shelf beside the stove and dump some coffee grounds in the water. I want to ask her about Jim, but don't dare with him sitting there. But I can tell by the calm way Mammy is rolling out the dough that Jim is still safe. Mammy will send word for him to come back when she's ready. Master won't let Mistress put the whip to Jim. Everybody knows that. About the only whipping there's going to be around here now is the one Death is putting on Mistress.

"What the doctor say?" Mammy asks as she cuts out the biscuits.

"Nothing while I was there."

I want to turn and see if he is staring at me like I want him to. But I keep my eyes on Mammy's bony black hands cutting circles from the white dough. I don't want to know how I would feel if he wasn't looking at me.

"Doc Carson is a good doctor, but even he can't beat ol' Death."

His voice is soft. It makes me think of horses grazing in a meadow in the springtime.

"I suppose not," I manage to say, turning

slowly to look at him.

He is looking at me and I'm ashamed, because I want him to and I don't want him to. He is looking at me and I know he can see through my thin dress and is looking at all the ugly scars and welts on my stomach and across my breasts. Mammy Sukey said that even if I did have babies one day I wouldn't be able to suckle them, not with breasts scarred and torn and flattened like mine.

"I'm Forrest Yates, the blacksmith." He smiles.

"How do you do?" I say, remembering my manners. "They call me Maria."

"That's a pretty name."

"Thank you." I'm smiling now, smiling too much, because what I really want to do is laugh. But you can't laugh when there's nothing to laugh about. That's what I want to do, though.

He stands up to go. "Thanks for the water, Mammy."

"You don't need to be thanking me, Forrest. I don't know what I can ever do to thank you. You be careful and don't let Jim do nothing that would jeopardize you. You hear me?"

"You needn't worry. Jim wouldn't do anything like that."

"You come back in an hour or so and I'll have a nice big breakfast for you. With her being sick and Master being in Richmond most of the time, I can cook up some of this good food for us." She laughs.

"Thank you," Forrest says, but he is looking at me.

"That is one nice young man," Mammy Sukey says after Mr. Yates leaves.

"Yes," I say, trying not to sound interested but hoping she keeps talking.

"He free."

"Free!" I exclaim. I understand now why he rides his horse slow, like he don't have nothing else to do.

"Born free. Never slaved a day in his life. But he cares more about us slaves than a lot of us do for ourselves. White folks think the world of him too. He's supposed to be the best blacksmith in Virginia. I heard Master say once that he wish he could find him a bootmaker to put shoes on his feet as good as the ones Forrest makes for horses."

"How did a black man get to be born free?" I want to know.

"His mama was Mistress Bradley's serving girl, and when Mistress Bradley died, she leave it in her will that his mama was to be set free. She was carrying Forrest at the time. He missed being born a slave by three months."

The water in the kettle is boiling now and I look at it, but it is only beginning to turn muddy. I like my coffee black.

"Hadn't you better get on back to the house to see if you needed? That coffee be here when you get back. You tell Master and the doctor that breakfast be ready in about twenty minutes, soon as these biscuits get done."

Forrest. That's perhaps the prettiest name I've ever heard in all my life.

"Did you hear me, girl?"

"Yes'm," I say quickly, hurrying from the kitchen, but once outside I stop and look toward the front of the house and then run across the road. The pines and oak trees and elm are silent and still in the early morning light. It is cool here in the forest. The birds sing and tiny animals run quickly on tiny feet across a floor of fallen leaves and pine needles.

2

Mammy Sukey says that you can tell how evil a person was by how long it takes them to die. Mistress must've been the Devil. She was all of three months dying, and if she had lasted five more days, she would've seen her thirtieth birthday.

But last evening after supper we heard the screech owl. That's always a sign of death. Yesterday morning a bird flew in the house. So we knew the end was near.

It was way up in the night when I was awakened by the sound of her thrashing in the bed. That wasn't anything new. The last month she thrashed around a lot, like she thought she could fight ol' Death off. She would thrash and curse. Cursed just about everybody in the state of Virginia, but especially her momma and poppa for getting themselves killed and leaving her alone to run a big plantation when she should've been putting on pretty dresses and going to balls in Richmond with handsome boys.

I listened to her cursing her momma and poppa for leaving her like they did, as if they wanted to or could help it. My momma and poppa left me, but I don't curse them. Maybe Mistress sold them because she wanted me to feel all alone like she did.

Last night she got to thrashing and cursing again, and then all of a sudden she started gagging and coughing and then breathing real heavy. It sounded like there was rocks and sand in her chest. She raised up in the bed and her hair looked like a dust rag with the moon shining on her. I was standing at the foot of the bed looking at her. She reached out her arms for me, but I didn't move. I knew Death had come in the room to stay this time. I didn't want her touching me as Death put his arms around her. Her eyes got big and they seemed to be calling my name. I didn't move. I just looked at her and then she fell back in the bed. I lay back down on the floor and listened to her breathing. It sounded like a big dog scratching at a door.

I didn't hear the quiet when it started. All of a sudden I noticed and it was like the whole world was still. I listened to the silence and wanted it to last forever. It felt like somebody was touching me all over with hands as soft as dandelion fluff. I didn't want to fall asleep, but I must have, because the first thing I know I am hearing the overseer ringing the bell. I get up and stand at the window until I see Forrest riding up through the slave quarter. I go out to the kitchen and tell Mammy.

"When did she die?" Mammy says sorrowfully.

"Just now."

"Poor thing."

I don't say anything, but go and tell the overseer. He stands a minute looking like Mistress's dying is an insult to him. He squirts tobacco juice on my feet and walks off to the slave quarter. It wouldn't be proper to have the slaves work in the fields until after her funeral. Overseer walk like he don't know what to do today with no slaves to whip.

When I get back to the house, Mammy has awakened Master. I bring him his breakfast in bed. There is no sadness in him. He sends me back to the kitchen for another helping of bacon and more biscuits. He says he wants to bury her this afternoon if Charles, the slave carpenter, can get a box made that soon. I tell him that folks might talk if he puts her in the ground so quick. He wants to know, What folks? She didn't have no kin and no friends. Won't be nobody to the funeral except Master and us slaves. The overseer be the only one to shed a tear, because he won't have a job soon. Least I hope not.

After I carry Master's dirty dishes back to the kitchen, Mammy and I go up to Mistress's room to wash her body and put her in her laying-out clothes. Her body is so smooth.

There are no marks on it, not even warts or pimples or birthmarks. Her breasts are round and big, and I don't know why, but I start crying and can't stop. Mammy puts her arms around me, thinking I'm sorrowing because Mistress is dead. But that's not it.

I run down to the stables, and when Forrest sees me, he puts down the bellows he's using on the fire and holds me close to him. I cry and cry, and feeling his big, strong hands on my back shames me so much, I break out of his arms and run and run until I cross the road and am in the forest. I lie down beneath a pine tree and cry and cry, and up in the tree I hear a squirrel squawking at me.

Mistress is laying in the box what Charles made. She is laying in the front parlor and there are big white candles at the head and foot of the box. Master stands at the head of the box in a black suit.

I stand in the doorway between the parlor and the dining room. The last of the slaves file past to pay their respects. They pass me on one side going in and on the other coming out. They look serious and sad as they file in, stop to look at Mistress, then shake Master's hand and say a few words to him. I'm the only one who sees the smiles on their faces as they go out.

Forrest comes in, Jim following. Master sees them and rushes forward to shake Jim's hand and to welcome him back to the plantation. You would think that Jim was his very own son. He's not. Master ain't like some slave masters who got a lot of back-door children. He just like Jim, 'cause Jim loves horses much as he do. He like Jim the way he like me. If Master like you, don't make no difference your color.

I wonder if Master knew that Jim was hiding at Forrest's house. Probably. Some other white man would've had Forrest arrested for hiding a runaway slave. Not Master. He know. He understand how it is.

The house is empty now. Master sits in a chair at the head of the box. It wouldn't be right for him to go up to bed and leave his dead wife all alone in the night. I don't think it's right for him to have to keep the death-watch all by himself, though, so I walk quietly across the polished floor and sit down by his chair.

He tells me that I can go to bed, but I say that's all right. I'd just as soon stay there with him. He don't say nothing for a long time. Maybe he's remembering, like I am, remembering the times he used to come to the house to court Mistress. I remember the second time he came and brought flowers to her and a paper sack of candy for me. He used to give me little notes to give her after he was gone.

We've known each other a long time, me and Master. He don't know much about me, I guess, but there ain't much to know about a little slave girl. Except I ain't little now.

I know a lot about him and I think he appreciate that I haven't ever told what I know. I didn't even tell Mammy when Master and Mistress stopped sleeping in the same bed, and that's been more than three Christmases ago. Even before that, I never told what they talked about in the night. We've known each other a long time, me and Master.

"Was there something I could've done different?" he asks me.

"No, Master. Not unless you could've brung her momma and poppa back to life. I think that's the only thing that would've made her different."

"And she made both of us suffer for it."

"She the one what suffer. We just hurt from time to time."

He don't say nothing for another long while. When he does, he says what I was afraid he would say.

"How would you like to come to Richmond and cook and wash for me? There won't be nothing for you to do around here anymore."

I look up at him. He has that shy man's look in his eyes, the way a man looks when the question he's asking is not the one he spoke. We've known each other for a long time, me and Master, and he ain't like a lot of masters are with the slave women. It ain't because he might not want to be. He just don't know how to do it and make it seem all right.

"That ain't a good idea, Master," I say.

"You're right, Maria," he says quickly, almost like he's glad I said what I did. "But what're you going to do now? I've been thinking about selling all the slaves and the house too. I'm not the man to run a plantation. And if I leave the overseer in charge, I'm afraid he'll whip everybody to death in a year's time."

"Yes, sir. But David Allman, the slave driver, know as much about running this place as Mistress did. In fact, whenever she had a decision to make, she didn't talk to the ol' overseer. She talk to David, even though he is a slave. He could run the plantation for you, and me and Mammy could help him."

He chuckles. "You and Mammy figure this one out together?"

"No, sir. It's my idea."

He laughs at that. "Maria, if you weren't a slave, there's no telling what you could've been."

"Yes, sir."

3

It has been a month since Mistress died. Before Master went back to Richmond, he told me that I could sleep in Mistress's bed and that I didn't need to do any work, except to see that everything was kept dusted and cleaned. I thanked him, but I moved into an empty cabin in the slave quarter. Mammy tried to shame me by saying I was scared to sleep in a dead woman's bed, but it's not that. I guess I'm just afraid that if I sleep in a soft bed too long, I won't know how to sleep on the floor when I get moved back there.

There is not much work. I dust and sweep and help Mammy in the kitchen. Master told her that it was all right for her to cook lunch to carry to the slaves in the field. Ol' overseer got mad about that, say Master's slaves eat better than white folks. I told him they ought to since they work harder. He turned so red I thought the blood was going to pop out of his face.

Mainly I wait for the evening. Forrest rides in about sundown. Sometimes I wait by the road and he'll ride up, reach down, and lift me on his horse. I'll wrap my arms around his waist and we'll ride to the top of a hill and watch the sunset.

Since that first morning when I walked into the kitchen and saw him sitting there, I don't suppose there's been a day when he hasn't come. I thought he was coming to tell Mammy how Jim was doing. She said I must be thick in the head not to know why he kept coming around.

That wasn't it. I know why I want him to come, but I don't know why he wants to come. He don't ever say and I don't ever ask. He comes and sometimes we sit in the kitchen and talk and drink coffee, or take a walk down by the creek. He tells me about all the different plantations he works on and all about the houses of the rich white people in Richmond and how he keeps their horses shoed and the wheels on their carriages repaired. I don't have much to say. I ain't never been anywhere and don't know nothing except what happens on this plantation. He don't seem to mind, though.

He's the most different man I've ever seen. He reminds me of Master. Forrest don't seem to be afraid of anything in the world. That must come from being born free. He can read and write and once he took a little twig and wrote my name in the dirt. He spelled out the letters to me, pointing to each one, and that was the most wonderful thing. I didn't see how them little up-and-down marks could be me, but it was wonderful anyway. He say that one day he'll teach me to read and write any word in the world. I shook my head and said that was more than I wanted. I didn't tell him that all I wanted was to learn to read and write his name. Then I'd go all over the world and write it on everything I passed. That would be a silly thing to do, but it feels nice to think about.

Master is back from Richmond. All us slaves are worried. We think he has made up his mind to sell us and get out of the slave-owning business. For three days now he has had me packing up all of Mistress's clothes and putting them in boxes, packing up the fine china and silverware. He's had some of the men slaves taking the best furniture to his new house in Richmond. All the while he look serious and don't talk except to give an order. Mammy said she tried to ask him what was going on, but he just told her that she would find out when the time came. We all know what that means.

The slaves what been taking the furniture to Richmond say that Master got a big, fine house there. They believe he must be going to marry again, 'cause wouldn't no single man need a house big as that. If that's true, then I'm not worried. I know Master wouldn't sell me or Mammy or Jim.

I've finished packing all of Mistress's belongings and I go to Master's study to tell him.

"I suppose you want me to put all them boxes in the barn tomorrow," I say, standing in the doorway and looking at him sitting behind his big desk.

"I don't reckon you'll be here tomorrow," he say, calm-like.

"Sir?" I say, feeling a large wound opening inside me. I blink my eyes rapidly, trying not to let him see me cry.

"I sold you today." He is smiling. I don't understand how he can say something like that and smile. I suppose his new wife-to-be told him to get rid of me and don't show no feeling about it.

"Yes, Master," I mumble. I notice my hands playing with the hem of my dress, like I'm some little baby.

"Your new master is waiting out back for you. I'm sure you'll be happy, Maria."

"Yes, sir." I stand there, waiting for him to say something else. I don't know what. Maybe that he's sorry or that he appreciates all I've done. But he lowers his head and goes to reading some papers on his desk.

"That's all," he says, looking up. But he's smiling. "Your new master is waiting for you."

"Yes, sir." I walk out of the study slowly and for an instant think about running out the front door, across the road, and into the forest. But I don't. I walk through the parlor and the dining room and out the back door.

I don't see anybody except Forrest, and I rush into his arms, sobbing. I don't want to tell him that I'll never see him again, but finally he quiets me and I tell him that I've been sold.

"Where's your new master?" he asks.

"Master said he was waiting for me out here." I look around but don't see anyone. "I don't see nobody."

"You don't?" Forrest asks.

I shake my head.

"I suppose I'm nobody," he teases me.

"Oh, you know what I mean," wondering how he can make a joke at a time like this. "Maybe Master meant to say that he was waiting in the front of the house."

We go to look, but there is no one there.

"Now, what exactly did your master say?" Forrest wants to know.

"He said I'd been sold and that my new master was waiting for me in the back."

Forrest takes my hand and we go around the house again. No one is there.

"I don't understand," I say.

"Well, your master wouldn't lie to you." He is smiling at me.

I'm about to lose my temper and ask him how come he think my being sold is so funny, when he starts to chuckle.

"You got to call me Master now," he say.

I can't believe it. "Forrest?" I say softly.

He has a grin on his face that's so big I'm afraid he's going to break his jaw.

"Forrest!" I shriek loud enough to wake the dead and all the angels in heaven. "Forrest!"

Laughing, he picks me up and whirls me around and around, and I'm laughing and crying and shrieking all at the same time. I still can't believe it, and when he puts me down, I demand that he tell me everything.

"Well, I went to him right after the funeral and asked him would he set you free because I wanted to marry you. He said he couldn't do that, because it was against the law. If he set you free, you would have to leave the state of Virginia. But he said there wasn't any law against a free black man owning a slave. Fact is, I know several who own their wife and children. By the law, they can't marry. But ain't no law say they can't live together as a family. They slaves on paper and that don't mean nothing. He said he had to go to Richmond for a while, and when he came back, he'd sell you to me. So pack your things, because you coming home with me tonight."

"Mammy! Mammy!" I scream, and run into the house, almost knocking Master down. "Oh! I'm sorry, Master. I didn't see you standing here in the doorway." Then I throw my arms around his neck and hug him so tight I get scared I might break his neck. "Thank you, Master! Thank you!"

He doesn't hug me back, and when I let him go, he is smiling. It's not his real smile, but more like the one he would give Mistress whenever there was company around.

"I'm going to miss you," he says.

"Yes, sir," is all I can say, and he knows that I won't miss him.

4

Forrest rises early. Sometimes he has to ride a ways to the plantation where he'll be working that day. He tells me to go back to sleep, that he's used to getting up and fixing his own breakfast and packing a dinner. Even after two years he tells me that. I tell him what I've been telling him for two years: He can get used to letting me do it.

So we do it together. He starts the coffee boiling on the cookstove while I start frying up some pork chops and put the potatoes in the hot ashes in the fireplace. He goes out to the barn to give the horse he's going to ride that day some fresh oats and to brush him. I watch him through the window, and every morning it's like that first time when I saw him riding up through the slave quarter, riding slow and easy, like he was brother to the sun. I sweep out the cabin and make the bed while he's down to the barn. By then the coffee is ready, and I pour two cups and take them down to the barn. We sit on the railing of the corral and watch the sun come up.

Our house is at the top of a small hill and I can almost see the plantation where I lived. Sometimes I see smoke rising from behind the stand of pine trees that blocks the big house from my view, and when I do, I know that Master and his new wife are back from Richmond and Mammy is cooking up breakfast.

Forrest asked me once if I missed the plantation. I asked him if he had lost his mind. It don't make no difference how good a master is, you still a slave. Time I said it, however, I knew I should've kept my mouth shut.

That's the one thing me and Forrest argue about sometime. He say if he set me free, we would have to leave Virginia. I say, Let's go. He say that he don't want to, that he got plenty of work around here. I tell him that a blacksmith can get work up North. He say he don't know nobody in the North and he was born and raised in Virginia and for me not to worry. He say that he has already made out his will, and in there it says that I'm to be free when he dies. He say that is how his mother got free. He ask me if I trust my old master. I tell him that I do. He say that Master has the will and Master knows I'm to go free. I tell him I understand, but I'd rest easier in my mind if I wasn't a slave on paper.

I don't want to think about that this morning. Forrest is going into Richmond today, and he say I can come to go shopping if I want. He's going to see a man who has a pretty horse for sale. We got three horses now. I don't see why we need another one, but Forrest loves horses. He say he want a fine new horse just to pull the new carriage he wants to buy for me. I tell him the wagon is good enough for me. He say I don't understand.

Forrest leaves me off at the dry-goods store while he goes to buy the horse. Now that I'm here, I wonder why I came. I look at all the people walking up and down the street and wonder where they came from and where they're going. It is hot and the dust hangs in the air like laundry put out to dry. I go in and out of stores, but don't buy anything. I could make better dresses when I was eight years old.

I am walking down the street when I see a large crowd. I go toward it, hoping it's the puppet show I happened on the last time I came to town. I look around eagerly at the crowd, thinking that I might see Mammy, Jim, or somebody from the plantation. I don't see any black people, however.

Suddenly the crowd starts applauding and hollering. I look toward the front. There on a stage is a long, tall white man. Standing next to him is a black girl who looks no older than I was when Forrest came and took me. Her head is bowed.

"Ladies and gentlemen!" shouts the thin

white man in a shrill voice. "Now this here is one of the finest girls you'll see in the state of Virginia. She has worked in the fields, but with the proper training can work in the house. Obedient, docile, and there's not a mark on her body." He looks at the girl and says, "Take it off!"

She looks at him, her eyes growing big.

"Don't be bashful now," he says, laughing. The crowd laughs. "Just pull it over your head like you do for all the young bucks."

The crowd laughs louder.

The girl crosses her arms over her breasts and moves away from the white man. He grabs her by the arm and snatches the top of her dress, pulling on it hard. It rips and falls to the floor. The crowd cheers loudly.

The girl doesn't know what part of her body to hide from all the eyes. The crowd laughs even more. The white man slaps at her arms and she lets them hang limply at her side.

"Gentlemen! Now, I ask you! Have you seen a finer bit of flesh on the market in the past year? I guarantee that you haven't. This girl here is good for anything you might have in mind."

That causes more cheering and clapping.

The man tells the girl to turn around, and when she does, he grasps her buttocks and squeezes them. He turns her to face the crowd again and puts his hand on her full breasts and squeezes. "Just as ripe as a cantaloupe off the vine with the dew still on it. Now, who'll make the first bid?"

"Five hundred!" someone in the front yells.

The girl is looking straight at the crowd now, the tears running down her face. I cannot tell for sure, but I think she is looking at me.

"Five fifty!" comes another shout.

Maybe if she looks at me, she won't cry. She'll know that we can't ever let them see us cry. If they see us cry, then we won't have anything left that's ours.

"Seven hundred!"

I guess she can't see me, because her shoulders heave as her tears become sobs. I walk away before I go up on that stage and slap her.

Forrest and I have our worst argument yet as we drive home, the shiny black horse tied to the back of the wagon. He's angry that I didn't have better sense, as he puts it, than to stay away from the slave market. I tell him that I got plenty sense, better than him 'cause I don't want more horses than I need.

"You just can't get rid of the slave mentality is what's wrong with you," he tells me.

I don't say anything, because if we keep talking, one of us is going to say something that we can't take back — ever. That's what made it so bad for Master and Mistress. They said things to each other that "I'm sorry" wouldn't make go away. They said things that the other one couldn't forget; and not being able to forget it, there was nothing to do but remember.

"I shouldn't have said that," Forrest says after a while.

"You right," I tell him.

"I'm sorry."

His voice is soft and sweet like a quiet rain in the middle of the night in the springtime. I want to stay angry awhile longer, but when he talks in that voice, well, something happens to me. Before I get all the way soft, though, I have to know. "What you mean by saying I got a slave mentality?"

I can tell that he doesn't want to answer when he says, "Aw, nothing. I just got hot under the collar. You had me scared."

"If you hadn't meant something, you wouldn't have said it. I ain't never known you to waste no words, Forrest Yates."

He sighs like he knows he's caught. "Let me put it this way. I want us to live as good as white people. That means we got to have the things that white people do. That'll prove that we're just as good as they are."

"And that's how come you bought a horse we don't need and are going to buy a carriage we don't need?"

"It'll prove that I'm as free as they are."

I want to tell him that it proves that he's a bigger fool than they are, but I don't. When you love somebody, you can think they're a fool sometime, but if you say it, you're the fool.

"Maybe having the slave mentality ain't all bad," I say finally.

"I didn't mean that, Maria," he apologizes.

"It's all right. The slave mentality sees white folk and their fine horses and big houses and pretty china and all like that. But we see that they ain't got no love. And that's all I got to say on it."

It is a few weeks before all our wounds heal. Forrest needs to see me look at him with my eyes all soft and warm, like he is the best man in the world. I need him to look at me, his eyes all glazed over. When he looks at me like that, the scars on my body disappear and my breasts stand round and firm.

So when he rides in one evening in a carriage, I exclaim and carry on like it's the prettiest thing I've ever seen in my life. He is so proud of it, and maybe he's right. Maybe a black man needs carriages and fine horses to feel that he's really free. Maybe he can't believe he's free unless he can see it. All I know is that I hope he didn't have to borrow too much money to pay for it.

But I don't say any of that. Instead I cook him a special dinner of chicken smothered with dumplings. Afterward we look at each other across the table and everything is all right again. I look at him, and if he doesn't know where the sun lives, nothing can convince me that he won't find its address.

He left early this morning and will be gone for a couple of days working on plantations in the southern part of the county. If Mammy was at the plantation, I would go stay with her. She's in Richmond at Master's house there, so I think I will make a new dress for when Forrest takes me riding in the carriage. That'll help him feel free too.

It is almost dusk when I hear a horse galloping up the road. I hurry to the door, wondering what Forrest is doing home so soon. It's not him. It's Master.

"Master!" I exclaim as he gets off his horse.

"Maria," he says, kind of flatlike.

"It sure is good to see you. This is a real surprise. If I had known you were coming, I would've made some of that apple cobbler I know you like."

He smiles weakly. "Thank you, Maria. Mind if I come in?"

"Oh, excuse my manners, Master. Come right in, please. Can I get you something to drink?"

He sits down at the table. "No, thank you."

I wonder how come he don't want to look at me, but looks over my shoulder and out the door.

"I'm not very good at this sort of thing," he says nervously. "I wish I knew the right way to tell you."

"What is it? Has something happened to Mammy?" I say quickly, understanding now. "You just sit right there, Master. I can be ready to come with you soon as I get my shawl and saddle one of the horses." I start out the door.

"It's Forrest," he says in a dull voice.

I stop and turn around slowly. "Forrest?"

"He's dead, Maria."

I look at him for a moment, then I laugh. "Dead? No, Master. He just left here this morning. Somebody told you wrong."

"He went down to the Simpson plantation, didn't he?"

I nod weakly, the tears coming to my eyes.

"Seems that he was shoeing one of their horses and Mr. Simpson's little boy was watching. He didn't know any better and he got a stick. He thought it would be funny to watch the horse jump around if he flicked some live coals on it. Forrest was kicked in the head and died instantly. A boy rode up from there to tell me, and I rode straight out here. I'm sorry, Maria."

I shake my head and laugh again. "No, Master. That ain't true. That just ain't true. IT AIN'T TRUE!" And I run out, past the barn and the corral and into the forest. Then I cry.

5

Master sent Mammy to stay with me these weeks since Forrest — I still can't say it. How can I believe he's dead when I feel him alive? I look out the window and see him walking to the barn and exercising the big black horse in the corral. I wake up a half hour before light and start to light the fire in the stove. Then I remember. There's no reason to get up or build a fire or do anything else.

Forrest is laying over there on the other side of the corral, and when it rains, I worry if he's getting wet. There was a frost a few nights ago, and I stay awake worrying about him being cold lying in that ground. Mammy says that it'll be best for me to leave him here, to go someplace where everything won't remind me of him. There ain't no such place. I look at the sky and that reminds me of him. I look at the earth and think of him. I can't go and leave him all alone out there in the ground.

Today Master is coming out from Richmond with Forrest's will. Today I'm free. I wish I wasn't.

It is early afternoon when Master arrives. I was listening for the sound of a horse. He arrives in a carriage, and behind him another white man driving a wagon. I guess it takes more than one white man to read a will.

The long, tall white man in the carriage looks familiar, but I can't place him. I guess I must've seen him on the street in Richmond once.

Master doesn't introduce him but sits down at the table. The long, tall white man stands by the door. Master speaks to Mammy but barely nods at me. You would almost think he'd come to tell me that Forrest was dead.

He reaches into his coat pocket and takes out some papers. "I guess I'll get right to the point. You understand what this paper is, Maria?"

"Yes, sir, Master. Forrest explained to me about his will and how he was giving me my freedom."

Master nods. "That's right. It's all in here. I won't bother to read it to you, because it's all in lawyer's talk. But Forrest gives you your freedom."

"That's what he told me."

"There may be a problem, however."

"What problem, Master?"

"The laws says that when a man dies, all the money he owes has to be paid to the people he owes it to. Now, it seems that Forrest owes a fair sum of money." He unfolds the paper and reads down it until he comes to the part he's looking for. "He borrowed money from the bank to buy two horses, a carriage, and a ton of oats that was delivered last week."

"That's right," I agree.

"Now, what all that means is that you're going to have to pay back all that money."

"I ain't got no money, Master. You know that."

"None at all, Maria?"

"No, sir, not unless I sell all the horses, carriage, and the oats."

"Well, you could sell two of the horses. They're paid for. But the bank that loaned Forrest the money is the real owner of the other two horses, the carriage, and the oats."

I look at him blankly, not understanding.

"I'm sorry, Maria." Master looks at me

sorrowfully. "I'm afraid that you're going to have to be sold, and the money from that will be used to pay off Forrest's debts and the interest on them."

"Oh, Master, no!" Mammy exclaims.

"But you just told me that the will says I'm to go free."

"I'm sorry, child. You can't go free if Forrest owes money. All of his property has to be sold to pay his debts. According to the law, you're the most valuable piece of property he owned."

I remember the other white man now, and the way he ripped off the slave girl's dress.

Mammy begins crying. "Master, you can't let them sell Maria. She's been like a daughter to you. Like a member of your own family." She is kneeling beside his chair, her hands clenched almost like she is praying to him. He looks over her and out the window, the color rising to his cheeks.

"Master! Master! Can't you pay off Forrest's debts for her? You got plenty money, Master. You could do that. And Maria, she could come to Richmond and work off the debt to you and then you could set her free. You could do that, Master! You don't want to see her stood up on the auction block and sold away to somebody who will abuse her. You got too good a heart to do that to her, Master!" Mammy is sobbing uncontrollably now.

I look at Master, waiting to hear what he

will say. He looks at me and his eyes flicker rapidly, as if he cannot look at me directly, as if he is afraid to know what he would feel if he looked at me without his eyes fluttering like the wings of a honeybee. Forrest looked at me like that when he was angry and ashamed at the same time.

If I ask Master, he'll say yes. That's what he's waiting for. He did the asking the other time, but he never asked really. I didn't know that I shamed him when I said no. He agreed with me so quickly that I didn't think any more about it. Maybe he didn't either until right now. He's got all the power today. If he just says right out that he'll pay Forrest's debts, he won't have the power no more. I will.

I go to Mammy, pulling her from the floor.

"It's all right, Mammy. It's all right. I don't want no new mistress whipping me because she see something in Master's soul he shamed to have there."

I look at him as I say it, and he drops his head. Suddenly he gets up, gives me a hateful look, and then with a jerk of his head tells the slave auctioneer that he can take me. He takes a rope from his pocket.

"You don't need to tie me," I tell him. "I ain't going to run away."

And I won't. I can see myself standing up on that platform, and when he tears my dress off, I won't cry. I'll stand up straight, and when the white men start cheering and applauding, I'll stare every one of them in the eye and make them stop. Won't many of them want to buy me, and whichever one does will wish he hadn't.

'Cause I know. I know now where the sun lives.

A Christmas
Love Story

One

Ellen held the oak-framed oval mirror in front of her and stared. She did not see the smooth, creamy-white skin, the gray-green eyes, or the brown hair that fell down her back like a silken waterfall. She looked instead at the dark-skinned man standing behind her, his face without a smile or frown.

"I can't do it, William," she said, lowering the mirror. "I'm sorry. I can't do it." Emotion made her voice even deeper and huskier than normal.

William put a hand on her shoulder and squeezed gently. "I know," he said softly. "I'm afraid too."

She turned and looked at him. "You are?" she asked, surprised.

"I'm not a fool," he responded with quiet seriousness.

His admission of fear was oddly comforting. If he had said otherwise, she would have been too alone. She would be alone enough during the next four days. One mistake by her, one false move or word, and they were caught. William was depending on her.

"I love you, William Craft," she said, turning around and hugging him to her. "And if we're both afraid, then we are stronger." She released him. "I'm ready now."

Ellen sat down in the straight-backed chair in front of the dresser, the mirror in her lap. William began cutting her hair patiently, snipping an inch away at a time, as if he hated what he was doing.

That straight hair had fooled him into believing she was a white woman the first time he saw her. When he learned she was a slave like himself, he could not believe it, though he should have. He had been a slave in Georgia all of his twenty-four years. It was not uncommon for slave owners to have children by black women. He had seen many, and no matter how white their skins, how gray, green, or light-brown their eyes, or how straight and smooth their hair, William always knew they were slaves like himself.

Why, then, had he not known that Ellen was a slave, too, that July day two years ago? He had happened to look up from the bureau he was sanding to see her walk slowly past the window. Was it the way she held her head level and steady on her slender neck? Was it the slow, almost leisurely way she had passed the cabinetmaker's shop where he worked? She looked like the favored daughter of a wealthy planter strolling to have tea at a friend's.

It was almost impossible for a slave not to bear the marks of his or her condition, no matter how much he or she hated it. Shoulders carried proudly would acquire at least a stoop eventually, and the eyes become furtive, flitting around in their sockets like tiny birds at the approach of a cat. He had seen that look, particularly in the slaves who worked harder than mules on the plantations. He supposed he was lucky that Dr. Collins, his owner, had hired him out as an apprentice to John Knight, a cabinetmaker, when he was fourteen. After a few years some of the wealthiest families in Macon were coming to the shop, asking him to make sideboards, tables, and bureaus. From the money he earned, two hundred dollars a year went to Dr. Collins. He was allowed to keep the remainder.

Having a skill, being paid for his labor, and the basic solitude of his work had kept him secreted from the crushing weight of slavery. Ellen had been spared, too, being a lady's maid and her mistress's favorite servant. She was also her mistress's half-sister.

William clipped more rapidly now as clumps of soft, fine hair dropped to her lap and onto the floor at his feet. It was as if remembering had rekindled his hatred at being a slave, and he expressed it by removing that hair whose softness he loved to feel beneath his hand, even as he hated the white man who had bequeathed this hair, the gray-green eyes, and the white complexion to this woman he adored, this woman who was his wife.

Quickly now he was done. He took a clothes brush and whisked the clipped hair from her shoulders and back. Moving around to look at her, he stared for a moment and, taking a comb from the top of the dresser, pushed the hair back.

"There." He nodded, satisfied. "Maybe I should have been a barber instead of a cabinetmaker." He chuckled.

Ellen raised the mirror and looked at herself. She did not think she looked any more like a man than when her hair had hung to her waist. But she was not sorry to be relieved of that hair of her father's, who had also been her owner and so never looked at her with any expression other than the frown he bestowed on all his slaves. Ellen was only sorry that William could not also change the color of her eyes and blacken her skin. But if that were possible, their plan would not work. For the first and last time in her life, she was glad her father had been a white man. At least she would be glad four days from now — if all went well.

She stood, brushing clumps of hair from her lap.

"You get ready," William told her. "I'll sweep."

Ellen smiled. She still marveled at William's ability to sweep a floor without raising a wisp of dust. That had been his first job at the cabinetmaker's — sweeping the floor of wood shavings, sawdust, nails, and dowels, and doing it without covering the finished and half-finished chairs, tables, and bureaus with dust and debris. How could she not have married a man who handled a broom like that? she wondered, laughing to herself. The few times she had ever tried to sweep, one would have thought a dust storm had gone through the room.

She went behind the screen standing in a corner of the room and began putting on the unfamiliar clothes. Did a man put on the trousers before the shirt, or vice versa? William put on his pants first, and for some reason always the left leg before the right. Once he had put the right leg on first, stopped, taken it off, and put the left leg on. She chuckled as she slipped her left leg into the pants.

"Well?" she asked tentatively when she finally emerged from behind the screen. "Do I look like a young white southern gentleman?"

William looked at her with a critical eye. The white shirt and dark suit fit her well, and when her disguise was complete, he believed, she would be able to pass for a man. He smiled. "I think it's going to work, Ellen. I think it's going to work."

She laughed sardonically. "If it doesn't, we're going to be sold so far into slavery that the Lord won't be able to find us on Judgment Day."

"How do the shoes feel?" he wanted to know.

"Better. I'm glad I practiced walking in them the past few nights, but I still don't understand how men ever get anywhere. It's like walking with fish traps strapped to my feet."

"Good," he said absentmindedly, still looking at her critically. "Now come over here and sit on the bed, and I'll finish making you into a cultivated young man on his way to Philadelphia with his manservant for medical treatment."

As he took the long swathes of white cloth from beneath the bed, he wondered again if it was an insane idea. It was, and that was its safety. He was glad that it had been Ellen's idea, because everything depended on her.

He wrapped a swathe of cloth around her right hand and wrist, then pulled it over her shoulder and back, tying it into a sling. "Is that too tight?"

She shook her head.

He took the other piece of cloth and wrapped it around her chin and over her head, covering her smooth and hairless cheeks, which would give her away as a woman. "Where's the hat?"

"Oh. I left it behind the screen."

William got the hat and placed it on her head. He handed her the mirror. "Well, what do you think?"

Ellen gazed at the unfamiliar face in the

mirror. "Well, if nothing else, I certainly look like I'm on Death's doorstep."

William took the black cravat from the dresser and tied it around her neck. Finally he reached into his coat pocket and handed her the green spectacles. She put them on.

"Your face is almost totally hidden now," William said, pleased. "People will see the spectacles and the bandages, but not you."

She raised the mirror and looked at herself again. "I hope so," she said softly. "I hope so. These next four days are going to be worse, I think, than the twenty-two years I've been in slavery."

"Don't think about it. Just think about being in Philadelphia on Christmas Day and having freedom for a Christmas present."

"Do I dare, William? Do I dare?"

"If we don't dare, we'll die as slaves."

She nodded slowly. "I know. But I couldn't go through with this if it were just for me."

"Nor I," he agreed.

"But I want children and I will not have our children born into slavery!" she flared suddenly. "I will not! To have children and see them sold away from us or us from them as you saw your mother, father, brother, and sister sold. I would kill any child I birthed into slavery."

William blew out the candle, knowing that light seen coming from the cabin of slaves at that time of night would arouse suspicion if anyone walking along the street happened to see it.

They sat on the edge of the bed, neither daring to sleep if they had been able. No more words were spoken. There was only the waiting now, and the night passed so slowly that Ellen began to wonder if God had commanded the sun not to rise. But when the sky changed from black to inky blue, she did not notice until William touched her arm.

Though the rim of the sun's orb had not yet cleared the horizon, the blue-black of first light quickly changed to a deep ultramarine, and through the window Ellen saw the shapes of the trees. When the shapes changed to the spare limbs and branches of oak and elm, William squeeezd her hand.

"It is time," he whispered.

Ellen would not release his hand. "William?" she said finally, her voice faint. She turned and stared into his face and then traced it gently with her fingertips — the eyebrows, the full lips, the thick mustache, which still tickled sometimes when they kissed.

"If — if something happens and I never see you again, I want you to know that I love you more than I have ever been able to say. Do you know that, William?"

"I know, Ellen. If something does happen, I'll find you — if not here, then in the life beyond. But I will find you, wife."

"I'll be waiting. Forever would not be too long to wait for you."

They kissed and held each other for a long moment before William broke the embrace. "We must go or we'll miss the train."

He put on his white beaver hat and took the two already-packed valises from beneath the bed. They walked softly to the door. William opened it and peered out. All was still. The trees were as stolid as tombstones.

"Come," he whispered.

Ellen didn't move, as tremors suddenly shook her body.

"What's wrong?" William asked sharply.

She burst into tears and put her arms around his neck, squeezing him so tightly that it hurt. He dropped the valises, pushed the door shut, and put his arms around her.

She was glad for his silence, loved him even more for knowing there were no words that could quiet the terror of this moment. There were no words that could reconcile her to the rage of having to literally steal their own lives. And if they failed? He would probably be sold to a plantation to work like a yoked ox until he died. And some white man would pay handsomely to use her for his pleasure, as her mother had been used.

Her sobbing stopped almost as suddenly as it had begun. "Come, William. It is getting late."

He opened the door and they stepped out, as softly as the dawn sending a warm band of red and orange across the eastern horizon. They tiptoed across the yard to the street, afraid that the slightest sound might awaken those who slept on the upper floor of the large white house on the corner where her half-sister-mistress lived with her family.

When they reached the sidewalk, William handed her her valise. There was nothing more to say, and as if to acknowledge that they were no longer Ellen and William Craft, but "Mr. William Johnson" and "his slave," they turned and walked in opposite directions toward the railroad station.

William walked quickly, afraid he might be recognized by some early riser. He and Ellen had asked for and been given four-day passes by their respective owners. It was not unusual for slaves to be given passes at Christmastime to go visiting, so his presence on the street so early would not be questioned. He and Ellen would not be missed even until they were safely in Philadelphia. But he was afraid of being detained for any reason, and was glad when he reached the station and boarded the Negro car where he had to ride.

Ellen walked slowly. She was surprised at the stillness and peace she felt now. Even if they were caught, she had walked across some invisible line, and no one could ever take this moment from her, the first moment of her life when she knew what it was to be free, to be walking along the street early on a quiet and peaceful morning. There was a slight chill in the air, but the sky was clear. The sun would warm the day. That was what it was like to go from slave to free woman. One minute she had been cold. Now she was warm. They could never take that from her.

As she neared the red-brick railroad station, she adjusted the hat atop her head and reminded herself that she was now William Johnson. She remembered all the white men she had seen, how they hooked their thumbs in the pockets of their vests, crossed their legs when they sat, flicked invisible bits of lint from coats and trousers with a flick of thumb and forefinger. It was little things like that that identified a man.

As she entered the station, she noticed the line at the ticket window, as William had predicted. The ticket seller would have no time for idle talk or questions. From behind the green spectacles she looked over the people in the station quickly, afraid there might be someone who would recognize her. There was no one.

"Two to Savannah," she said when she got to the window, glad once again that her natural speaking voice was deep.

The ticket seller did not look up but reached beneath the counter, took two tickets, stamped them, and shoved them beneath the window grill. She pushed the money toward him and walked away.

William saw her as she emerged from the station house. Only when he heard the loud sigh escape his body did he realize how tense he was. Ellen did not look toward the back of the train, where the Negro car was, but proceeded slowly along the platform and entered the third car from the front.

William sighed again. Now, if the train would only start moving. He stared at the people coming out of the station house and pausing on the platform to say good-bye to friends and relatives. Just then someone rushed out, pushing and shoving his way through the crowd. William almost leaped from his seat, and his heart was pounding as loudly in his ears as the hammer with which he had pounded so many nails.

There, hurrying toward the train, was John Knight, the cabinetmaker for whom he worked. A tall, lean man with a sharp nose like a rooster's beak, Knight stopped a white man, speaking rapidly while pointing at the train. The man shook his head and Knight walked quickly toward the train.

William snatched the white beaver hat from his head and put it on the seat beside him, cursing to himself. There were some whites who seemed to have some kind of sixth sense about their slaves, and John Knight was one. He hadn't wanted to give William the pass.

"What do you need a pass for?" he'd asked. "You see your wife every night. I could understand if she lived on one of the plantations in the countryside."

"Yes, sir," William said, seeming to agree. "That's just it. My wife and I would like to go visit her mother, and since I've never asked you for a pass, sir, I didn't think you'd mind this once, sir."

Though William had kept his eyes looking downward in the proper pose of submission, he could almost feel Knight thinking. White men lived in fear of slaves escaping. Any request a slave made was scrutinized for hidden means of running away.

"Well," Knight began finally, "I better see you bright and early the day after Christmas. If I don't, I'll have the slave catchers after you so quick you'll wish you'd never been born."

Now here he was, entering a coach of the train, the one, William realized, where Ellen sat! William waited, scarcely breathing, and though only a moment passed, it seemed like hours before Knight walked off the coach and hurried to the next one. Quickly he was off that coach and leaped up the steps to the next. Two more coaches and he would come to the last one, the Negro coach.

"We are caught," William mumbled, and angry tears moistened his eyes as he pounded his fist on the coach seat. And almost in response to the blow the train jolted once, twice, a third time, and slowly began moving. William saw Knight jump from the train, and though he wanted to frame his face in the window for Knight to see, William shrank down in the seat. It was some moments before he dared rise up again.

Ellen had not seen Knight when he entered the car. She was gazing through the window, wondering why, at the moment of leaving, there were these unwanted feelings of sadness. She couldn't believe that she would really miss Rebecca. But why shouldn't she? They were half-sisters, weren't they, and looked so much alike that many white people used to comment to Rebecca's mother about her "two lovely daughters." That was why Rebecca's mother had wanted to sell Ellen as far away from Georgia as possible. For some reason it had never happened. Eventually, though, she got rid of Ellen, giving her to Rebecca for a wedding present as if she were a bowl of cut crystal, or a place setting of silver.

Foolishly, Ellen had expected her half-sister to free her. Instead, Ellen continued to wait on Rebecca as she had since she was seven and Rebecca ten. Ellen awakened her in the morning, took out the chamberpot, carried warm water from the kitchen for her to wash with, made the bed, laid out her clothes, mended her dresses and underwear, sewed new clothes for her, brushed her hair, as long and brown as Ellen's, and listened to her chatter about the "ball at the Markham plantation," and "dinner with the Bells in Atlanta."

Once a day Rebecca would hug Ellen, exclaiming, "Oh, Ellie! You're my dearest friend in all the world! I don't know what I'd do without you!"

"Learn to mend your own drawers," Ellen had wanted to tell her so often.

Now, as she felt the train gathering speed, she knew that her sadness had nothing to do with leaving her half-sister, who would've sold her if she had ever needed the money.

No matter how right it was for her to leave, her emotions knew only that they were being carried into the new and the unknown. Afraid, they clawed to cling to the known, no matter how horrible.

When the city of Macon passed from her window to be replaced by the flat, red clay countryside, Ellen turned and was surprised she hadn't noticed that someone had taken the seat next to her. Out of the corner of her eye she saw something familiar. It appeared to be a walking stick whose knob was artfully carved into a face — a carved face she had looked at only three nights ago when Mr. Cray, a cotton dealer from Savannah, had come for dinner with Rebecca and her husband.

Ellen was afraid she was going to faint, or worse, cry out. Was it just coincidence that Mr. Cray was on the same train? But coincidence would not have placed him beside her. How could he have found out? She and William told no one.

Ellen turned to look through the window again, biting her lip to hold back the tears.

"It is a very fine morning, sir," Ellen heard Cray's rich bass voice.

Was he addressing her? she dared wonder.

"I said it's a fine morning, isn't it, sir?" Cray's voice repeated, louder.

He was addressing her, wasn't he? Ellen thought.

"I'll make him hear," Cray said, insulted

and annoyed now. "It is a very fine morning, sir!" His voice reverberated the length of the coach.

Ellen knew she had to do something, but if she turned and he recognized her, it was over! Yet, what if she looked him directly in the eye and spoke, and he saw a man?

She turned her head and found his eyes staring into hers. "Yes, it is a fine morning," she said, making her voice even deeper. "I hope you will excuse my hearing," she continued, then smiled, and turned back to look out the window again, her heart fluttering as rapidly as the wings of a hummingbird.

"It's a terrible thing to be deaf," she heard someone behind her whisper to Mr. Cray.

"It certainly is," he returned sympathetically. "I won't trouble that young man anymore."

Ellen didn't relax, however, until the train stopped at the next town and Mr. Cray got off.

It was evening when the train arrived in Savannah. As William put on his white hat and walked off the car, he could smell a heavy saltiness to the air. That could only be the ocean, he concluded, though he had never smelled it before.

He walked slowly forward to the car where his "master" was. When "he" descended the steps, William did not look up into that face he loved so completely, but with one hand reached for "his" hand, while taking the suitcase from "him" with the other. As Ellen stepped onto the station platform, she squeezed William's hand before releasing it.

"Were you able to rest, Master?"

"I'm afraid not, William."

"Perhaps you'll be able to sleep tonight on the steamer."

"I hope so."

The station platform was crowded with disembarking passengers and friends and family who'd come to meet them. It was Christmastime, Ellen remembered, a time for reunions and cheeriness. Or so she had observed.

She wondered why William was standing there holding the valises. Then she remembered. She was the "master" and had to find the carriage to take them to the dock to the steamer for Charleston, South Carolina.

She started slowly across the platform and through the station, William a discreet two paces behind. Once on the street, a man standing beside a carriage stepped forward quickly.

"Going to the Charleston steamer, sir?"

Ellen nodded. "Yes."

"Right this way. That your nigger?"

"Yes, he is. And a more faithful servant cannot be found in all of Georgia."

The man opened the door of the carriage. "Well, consider yourself blessed by God."

"I do," Ellen responded, smiling to herself as William took her hand and squeezed it tightly as he helped her inside.

"You can ride up top with me, boy," the carriage driver told William.

As the carriage moved slowly through the streets of Savannah, William wished it had been daylight so he might see something of this city by the ocean. It was a place favored by many wealthy whites, especially at this time of year, when the weather might turn chilly in central Georgia. He'd overheard whites in the cabinet shop talk of plants and trees growing in this city that must be wondrous to see — palm trees, oak trees with hanging moss. It was odd to be in a place and not know exactly where he was.

If whites had not talked so casually around him at the shop and around Ellen at Rebecca's, as if slaves did not have ears or brains, they would not have known what to do. But by putting together the conversations they had overheard so many times, they learned how to travel from the South to the North and freedom. At least he hoped they had.

When they arrived at the wharf, William leaped down and opened the door to assist his "master." While he took the valises, Ellen paid the driver. They walked up the gangplank in silence, and William waited nervously while his "master" bought the tickets. The ship's captain directed the ill-looking "white man" toward "his" cabin.

Once inside, Ellen threw her free arm around William and they clung to each other for a moment.

"How are you?" William wanted to know.

"Good, I suppose," she said, weariness in her voice. "I had a frightful scare though," and she told him about her encounter with Mr. Cray.

William related the sudden appearance of Mr. Knight and the train's fortuitous departure before he got to the Negro coach.

"Well, with two narrow escapes like that, do you suppose it could be an omen?" she wanted to know.

"I hope so."

Ellen sank down onto the bed. "Could you take the sling off?"

William shook his head. "I don't think that's a good idea. What if something happens and someone comes in the middle of the night and you don't have it on?"

She sighed. "You're right. But my arm is so stiff, I wonder if I will ever have feeling in it again."

"Once we're in Philadelphia, I'll kiss it back to life," he said, smiling broadly.

"William Craft!" she exclaimed, laughing and blushing.

"I love you, wife," he said, kissing her softly. "Now, it's about time for you to go down to supper, isn't it?"

She shook her head. "Not tonight, William. I just don't think I could carry off being the young slave owner tonight."

"But you haven't eaten all day," he protested.

"I'll be fine," she reassured him. "Sleep is what I need."

"Very well. I'll see you at breakfast."

"Must you go so soon?"

"It's best not to arouse suspicion."

She nodded. "Be careful, husband."

"I will."

When William returned to the deck, he was surprised that he could not see the wharf. It took him a moment to realize that the ship was moving. How could that be? To move and not feel the motion. Was this what it felt like to be a white, fluffy cloud on an endless blue sky?

He stood at the rail for a moment, looking out into a black nothingness that he knew was the ocean. What did it look like? He couldn't imagine water so wide that there was nothing else to be seen. So dark was it, he would've thought that he had become a star against the night if he had not been able to see the stars above him.

The breeze carrying the smells of the unseen ocean was chilly now, and just as he was wondering where the colored passengers slept, the captain came up to him.

"Your master didn't look too well, boy," he said roughly.

"No, sir. He sick." William deliberately responded with the poor grammar expected of him.

The captain laughed harshly. "You'd have to be blind not to see that. What's wrong with him?"

"He sick, sir," William said, grinning. "I don't know he sickness."

"Well, I just hope he doesn't die on my boat."

"Massa die?" William exclaimed, laughing. "Aw, sir. Massa not gon' die. No, sir! He just don't look so good right now, because of all the traveling. That's all, sir."

The captain nodded. "Hope you're right," he said, and turned to walk away.

"Begging your pardon, sir?" William called after him.

The captain stopped and turned around. "What is it?"

"Where is the place the niggers sleep at?"

The captain laughed. "Boy, you know how to sleep on your feet, don't you? That's all niggers good for anyway. Sleeping and eating. Ain't no cabins on my boat for niggers." Laughing loudly, he walked away.

William walked the deck until he saw a pile of cotton sacks lying near the steamer's funnel. It was warm there and he lay down, placing his hat beside him. As tired as he was, he did not sleep, but gazed into the night sky. He remembered when he was a child, before his parents were sold. He rememberd the summer nights he stared up and into the night as he was doing now. It had made him feel that he wasn't a slave anymore, but just a little boy wondering why the stars did not fall out of the sky. He remembered wondering why he had been born a slave and not a star.

He wasn't a child any longer, but he wondered still, not only about that, but if the stars could see him as clearly as he saw them. Did he twinkle in the night to their eyes as they did to his?

When the sun rose, he got up and went to the rail to look at the ocean. He was disappointed that it looked scarcely different from a large, wrinkled piece of cloth. Unlike the night sky, which made him wonder about himself and the world, the ocean was simply there. It did not twinkle or brood. It just lay there.

He did not know how much time passed before he heard voices. He walked into the dining hall. Five men were sitting down to breakfast. William moved forward quickly to help his "master," who was just taking a place next to the captain.

"You seem to be feeling better this morning," the captain said to Ellen.

"Yes, thank you."

"I hope your ailment is not serious."

"I don't think so. My doctor believes it to be an attack of inflammatory rheumatism," she added, using a term she'd overheard once from one of Rebecca's dinner guests. "He recommended that I see a physician in Philadelphia."

Breakfast was served and William leaned over to cut his "master's" food into small pieces.

"Will there be anything else for now?" William asked.

"No, William."

As soon as he returned to the deck, the captain said, "You have a very attentive boy, sir. But you had better watch him like a hawk when you reach Philadelphia. I know several gentlemen who have lost valuable niggers in the North."

Before Ellen could muster a reply, a man sitting opposite, with a long mustache that curled downward to the corners of his mouth, both elbows on the table, a large chicken breast in his hands, and a fair portion in his mouth, spluttered, "Good advice, Captain. Very good advice." He dropped the chicken breast into the plate and leaned across the table, staring intently at Ellen. "I would not take a nigger to the North under any circumstances. I have dealt with many niggers in my time. I never saw one who put his heel upon free soil that either didn't run away or amounted to a hill of beans when he came back to these parts." He picked up the piece of chicken. "Now, sir, if you wanted to sell that nigger of yours, I'm the man to talk to. Name your price, and if it's reasonable, I'll put the silver dollars on the table right this minute."

The man took a large bite out of the chicken breast, but his eyes did not waver from Ellen's face. She forced herself to meet his gaze, though she felt she was staring into Death's very own face.

"I do not wish to sell, sir," she said calmly. "I cannot get on well without him."

The man snorted. "You'll do without him pretty quick if you take him to the North. I have seen lots of niggers in my time, and I guarantee you that that is a keen nigger. I can see from the cut of his eye that he is certain to run away. You'd better sell him to me and let me put him on the market down in New Orleans."

"I think not, sir," Ellen responded firmly. "I have great confidence in his fidelity."

"Fi*devil*!" the slave trader exploded, banging his fist on the table and accidentally catching the edge of his saucer, sending the cup of hot coffee spilling into the lap of the man seated next to him. The scalded man jumped up with a sudden shriek.

The slave trader patted him on the arm. "Sit down, neighbor," he said brusquely. "Accidents will happen in the best of families." Then, pointing his finger directly at Ellen, he continued, "It makes me mad to hear a man talking about fidelity in niggers. There isn't a one who wouldn't run away, given a chance. If I was President of these United States, I wouldn't let any man take a nigger into the North and bring him back to the South. These are my flat-footed, every-day, right-up-and-down sentiments. I am a southern man, every inch of me to my back-bone."

Suddenly the men at the table stood, shouting, "Three cheers for the sunny South! Hooray! Hooray! Hooray!"

Alone in the midst of the raucous yells

stood a portly, balding man, the front of his trousers wet and stained with coffee. Ellen thought he looked as if he wanted to cry, and when he noticed the "young gentleman's" look of sympathy, he smiled gratefully.

Just then someone opened the dining-room door and announced that the steamer was approaching Charleston harbor. The men dispersed and Ellen returned to the cabin, grateful to find William waiting for her there.

"That was an ordeal!" she exclaimed after they embraced.

"The noise had me a little nervous."

Ellen chuckled. "Oh, they were worried about your fidelity, William. You aren't going to get up North and fall in love with some fancy northern girl, are you?"

"What are you talking about?" he asked, bewildered.

Suddenly her body slumped and William held her to him. "I was just trying to make a joke before I became hysterical," she said weakly.

"Three more days," William whispered.

"Three hundred years would not seem so long."

Knowing there would be a crowd at the dock, William and Ellen were afraid to disembark immediately, fearing they might be recognized, or that Knight had acted on his suspicion and telegraphed a message for the authorities to be on the lookout for them.

The wharf was practically deserted when they finally left the boat, William holding

Ellen by the arm. A carriage took them to the hotel, one which Ellen had heard Rebecca mention as the best in Charleston.

Ellen rested through the day. That evening she and William returned to the wharf for the next part of their journey.

"A ticket for myself and my slave to Philadelphia, sir," Ellen told the ticket agent.

The agent's face was the color and texture of cheese, and he scowled through the grill. "Boy!" he yelled suddenly at William, who stood to the side.

"Sir?" William responded quickly.

"Do you belong to this gentleman?"

"Yes, sir!"

The agent turned back to Ellen. "You have to register your name here, sir, the name of your nigger, and pay a dollar duty on him."

Ellen paid the dollar and, pointing to her bandaged hand, said, "As you see, I am not able to write." This was literally true. She was glad now that she had thought of having her arm and hand bandaged. Nothing would have given them away as escaping slaves more quickly than the inability to write. "I would be grateful if you would sign for me, sir."

The agent shook his head vigorously. "I won't do it! No, sir! I won't do it!"

Ellen wondered if he suspected something. Or was he one of those people who enjoyed being contrary? Whatever his motive, it didn't matter. What would she do if he continued to refuse? Would it be something ridiculous like this that would lead to their undoing?

Just then a man with a round, pudgy face and wearing a top hat walked up to Ellen, smiling. "Having a problem?" he asked warmly, patting Ellen on the back.

For an instant Ellen was confused. Then she recognized the man on whom the coffee had been spilled that morning. She smiled warmly.

"The ticket agent says I must register my slave, but as you can see, my infirmity prevents me from writing, and the agent will not do the writing for me."

"Nonsense!" the man exclaimed. "See here, sir!" he continued, pointing his finger at the ticket agent. "I know this young man's people. Good family. One of the best in the South. Now, kindly enter his and his slave's name in the register so he may be on his way."

Ellen couldn't believe what she was hearing. Why was he telling such a lie? Was he that grateful for the look of sympathy she had given him as he stood at the table looking very foolish and alone?

The ticket agent appeared confused now, and looked over his shoulder at someone Ellen could not see.

"That's good enough for me, Eli." Ellen heard a voice, then saw the captain of the steamer come into view. "I will register the gentleman's name and take the responsibility myself."

Ellen thanked the captain and her companion from the boat warmly, and William moved forward quickly to assist his "master" from the terminal and onto the steamer.

Once the steamer was under way, the captain came to Ellen and explained. "I hope that you will not take what happened as a sign of disrespect, Mr. Johnson. They make it a rule to be very strict at Charleston. I have known families to be detained there with their slaves until reliable information could be received respecting them. You know, it would be mighty easy for an abolitionist to come down here, pose as a slave owner, and take off a lot of valuable slaves."

"Yes, you're quite right," Ellen agreed. "Quite right. I appreciate your assistance more than I can say."

William slept fitfully that night, curled in a corner of the deck near the funnel. He awoke often, however, not only concerned that they had come closer to being caught, but worried even more about Ellen. If his own nerves were frayed, Ellen's must be near to unraveling.

"Only two more days," he whispered through the night to her. "Two more days, my love."

The steamer reached Wilmington, North Carolina, after breakfast the next morning. William and Ellen transferred without incident to the train for Richmond, Virginia.

Ellen settled wearily onto the lumpy train seat. She had thought by now she would be accustomed to her role. But the closer they came to freedom, the more nervous and frightened she was. How much worse to be caught now than at the beginning. And the closer they came, the more she doubted that they would succeed. How could they? How could everyone not see there was a woman behind the bandages and green spectacles?

But maybe there was something about her that looked like a man. She wanted to take her mirror from the valise and look at herself closely to reassure herself that there was something womanly about her. She needed William to tell her how beautiful she was. When these four days were ended, she would want to hear him tell her that for the next 40,000 days, and then make him begin again.

A young woman and a man with a full and neatly trimmed black beard sat down in the seat across from her. The woman looked to be only a year or two younger than Ellen, and with her sparkling blue eyes and cheeks flushed red from the morning chill, she was quite lovely.

Though Ellen didn't want to talk, she found herself in yet another conversation about the bandages and her "health." The young woman chattered a little too eagerly, Ellen noticed, her cheeks flushing red long after the chill should've left them. When the young woman shyly and gravely offered "Mr.

Johnson" an apple, her eyes cast downward, Ellen couldn't help blushing. The girl was attracted to William Johnson!

Ellen thanked the girl warmly, and didn't know what else to say, embarrassed for herself and the girl who was being deceived. Ellen pleaded fatigue, closed her eyes, and pretended to sleep.

After some moments Ellen heard a deep sigh.

"Papa, Mr. Johnson seems to be a very nice young gentleman." She sighed again. "I have never felt so much for a gentleman in my life!"

Ellen was greatly relieved when the train came to the next stop and she opened her eyes to see the man and his daughter preparing to get off.

The girl's father handed Ellen his card. "The next time you are traveling this way, Mr. Johnson, I would be honored if you would do us the kindness of calling on us. I would be pleased to see you." Smiling, he added, "I believe my daughter would be too."

The girl's face turned a deep red. "Oh, Papa!" she exclaimed. Then, trying to muster her dignity, she looked at "Mr. Johnson" and said solemnly, "It has been a pleasure meeting you, and I will pray for your health."

"Thank you," Ellen said, holding the card in her hand, afraid to cast a glance at it for fear that she might be holding it upside down and would not know. Only when the man and his daughter had left the train did Ellen put the card in her pocket.

The ride from Richmond to Fredericksburg, Virginia, was quiet, and Ellen slept. A little beyond Fredericksburg she and William transferred without incident to the steamer for Washington, D.C.

Only two more changes, Ellen thought, as she settled into a chair on the deck. Maybe they were going to make it.

Perhaps she was more optimistic because, for the first time in three days, she was able to share part of the trip with William. He was leaning against the rail at the other end of the deck. He looked so handsome in his black suit, black cravat, and white beaver hat. When she'd seen it in the store window in Macon, she had insisted he buy it. He had been afraid it would attract too much attention on the trip. She wanted him to dress as handsome as he was, and he was the most wonderful sight she had ever seen.

"Sir!"

The harsh voice was at Ellen's shoulder, and though it startled and frightened her, she willed her body not to tremble.

"I am speaking to you, sir!"

She turned slowly to look into the angry face of a thin man peering at her through wire-rimmed spectacles. "Sir?" she responded with a coolness she couldn't feel.

"Is that your nigger?" he asked, pointing at William.

She inclined her head in a curt nod.

"What are you trying to do?" the man sputtered, spittle flecking his lips. "Spoil him by letting him wear such a fine hat? Just look at the quality of it. The President couldn't wear a better hat. If I had my way, I'd go and kick it overboard."

A man sitting a few chairs away came over and said mildly, "Come, come, my good fellow. Don't speak in such a way to a gentleman."

"And why not?" the thin man shouted, his tiny eyes bulging. "It makes me itch all over, from head to toe, to get hold of every nigger I see dressed like a white man. That nigger ought to be sold to New Orleans and have the Devil whipped out of him."

Ellen rose quickly but calmly. "Please excuse me, gentlemen." She walked to her cabin, where she fell across the bed, her body trembling, as she bit her lip to hold back the sobs that wanted to escape from her body.

There was a knock on the cabin door. She sat up, but was afraid to know who was on the other side.

The knock came again. "Master?"

"Oh, thank God!" she sobbed, hurrying to unlock the door and admit William. "Thank God!" she repeated, clinging to him.

"It's almost over," William said softly. "It's almost over."

When the boat docked at Washington, they transferred quickly to the train for Baltimore, the last major slave port before they would enter the North.

It was night when the train arrived in Baltimore. The station was crowded with people arriving and leaving, carrying baskets with brightly wrapped presents.

It's Christmas Eve, William remembered, but he did not pause to look at the large Christmas tree in the station, its boughs holding tiny lighted candles. He knew that Ellen would not endure much longer, and he could feel her body trembling as he guided her through the station and onto the train for Philadelphia. There were too many people around to risk whispering to her, but he squeezed her upper arm tightly as he helped her to a seat.

As he came off the train and made his way to the Negro car, a white-haired man in a gold-braided uniform stopped him. "Where are you going, boy?" he asked sternly.

"Philadelphia with my master, sir," William replied, the quiet calm in his voice hiding the rising fear that something was wrong.

"Where is your master?"

"In the carriage I just left, sir." William smiled.

"You'd better get him out," the station-master said firmly. "And be quick about it! No man can take a slave past Baltimore unless he can prove that he has the right to take him along. Get him off now and bring him to my office."

William watched the stationmaster walk into the terminal. He didn't know what to do. He had never overheard any slave owner in Macon speak of needing proof of slave ownership to go from the South to the North. Maybe he should quietly disappear now. Ellen would be free, at least, and he would take his chances of finding his own way.

But if he just disappeared, Ellen would never know what had happened to him. He couldn't do that to her. Slowly he stepped back onto the train and saw Ellen sitting alone at the far end of the coach. She looked up and smiled when she saw him. He managed a weak smile, wondering how he was going to tell her.

"How are you feeling?" he whispered, leaning over the seat.

"Much better." Her smile was radiant. "We did it, William."

"Not quite," he said solemnly. Quickly he told her what had happened.

"No!" Ellen exclaimed loudly, then lowered her voice. "No, no, no!"

William feared she was going to dissolve into uncontrollable sobbing as she kept repeating, "No, no, no! No, William; No!"

They were less than twelve hours from Philadelphia and freedom. They couldn't have come so close to be stopped now. Could they?

William grasped her hand. "Let's go," he said gently.

"Go where?" Ellen demanded to know. "What are we going to do?"

"I don't know. Let's go to the office."

She gripped his hand fiercely. "You aren't going to trick me, are you, and run off or do something foolish? I don't want freedom without you, William Craft."

"No. Let's go to the office. We've come this far. I just can't believe that we are not meant to go all the way."

The stationmaster's office was crowded with travelers exchanging holiday greetings with the white-haired man seated behind the large desk at the end of the room. Ellen noticed the bottle of liquor on the edge of the desk, and the glasses of amber-colored liquid in the hands of the dozen or so men jammed into the tiny room. She noticed, too, that the sounds of joviality diminished as she and William made their way through the crowd. There was only silence when she and William stopped before the stationmaster.

"Did you wish to see me, sir?" she asked, her voice tiny and barely audible in her ears.

"Yes, I did," the stationmaster said. "It is against the rules of this railroad, sir, to allow any person to take a slave out of Baltimore and into Philadelphia unless he can satisfy us that he has a right to take him along."

Ellen looked at the stationmaster, at the white hair and pale blue eyes that looked at her kindly. He was just an old man doing his job anxious for the train to leave so he could get home to spend Christmas Eve with his family. There wouldn't be any problem, she was sure.

"And why is that, sir?" she asked, her voice strong now. "Isn't the word of a white gentleman worth anything in Baltimore?" she asked indignantly.

The pale soft eyes of the stationmaster hardened so quickly that Ellen was startled, and when he spoke, his voice was so cold, Ellen could feel the warmth leaving her body. She had made a mistake, a fatal one.

"Sir, a gentleman would not question the rules of this railroad or the laws of this great city. But if you are so dense that you don't understand, let me explain. If we allowed any gentleman to take a slave past here into Philadelphia, and should the gentleman not be that slave's rightful owner, and should the lawful owner come prove that his slave escaped on our railroad, the railroad would have to pay that man what he said his slave was worth. And that money would come out of my pocket! Now do you understand?" he asked with sarcastic finality.

Ellen felt the eyes of everyone in the room on her. Suddenly there was the sound of a chuckle.

"Now, now, Arnold," someone said to the stationmaster. "That's not the proper Christmas spirit, is it?"

"Hear, hear," came another voice. "Arnold, you can plainly see the state of the gentleman's health. A gentleman in his condition needs his faithful servant."

"Furthermore," came a third voice, "you

don't really think a nigger would try to run away by riding the train, do you?"

Everyone laughed at such a ridiculous idea.

"All I know," countered the stationmaster, "is that if a nigger escapes on one of my trains, the railroad will hold me responsible. A nigger like that one there probably goes for a thousand dollars. And that's a thousand dollars I don't have."

It was an argument none of the men could refute.

"Sir," one of the men said, addressing Ellen, "isn't there someone in Baltimore who can vouch for you and your slave?"

"No. I am a stranger passing through to seek medical treatment in Philadelphia." Ellen looked at the stationmaster, who was pouring himself another drink. "Sir, I bought tickets in Charleston to pass us through to Philadelphia. Therefore you have no right to detain me here. None whatsoever!"

The words were not out of her mouth before she knew she had made another mistake. But she hadn't gotten this close to be stopped! The man had to be made to change his mind.

The stationmaster leaped up from behind the desk. "Right or no right!" he shouted. "I will not let you pass!" His face flushed red, and his arm trembled as he pointed at her and shouted even louder, "I will not let you pass!"

Everyone in the room seemed frozen. No one moved or spoke or even dared breathe, it seemed. Ellen knew that she was supposed to turn and walk out. She would have had she been able to. But she couldn't move. To turn and walk out was the end.

So she stood and stared at the station-master. He stared back. Leave, she told herself. Leave. There might be another way to Philadelphia. Maybe William was right. She could go ahead and, once in Philadelphia, find some means to locate him and help him escape.

If she didn't walk out soon, the station-master would summon the police to eject her and maybe arrest her even. And that would be the worst thing that could happen. Leave!

But she could not move. The only sound in the room was the tick-tick of the pendulum of the tall clock behind the stationmaster's desk.

The door of the office opened. Certain that the police had been summoned somehow, Ellen turned. But she had scarcely moved before she noticed that it was only the conductor who'd been on the train from Washington to Baltimore.

He sauntered in, laughing when he saw the bottle sitting on the stationmaster's desk. "Just the thing I was looking for, Arnold," he said brightly.

"Did these two ride in with you from Washington?" the stationmaster asked abruptly, pointing to Ellen and William.

Someone handed the conductor an empty glass and he poured himself a drink. He turned and looked at Ellen and William.

"These two?" he asked, swallowing the drink quickly. He chuckled and wiped his mouth with the back of his hand. "Now, that'll keep me warm for a while." He set the glass on the desk and, nodding at Ellen and William, said, "Come in from Washington same as I did. Come all the way from Macon, Georgia, believe he said. Going to Philadelphia to see some doctor up there."

Just then the bell rang, announcing that it was time for the train to leave. "Well, time for me to go to work," the conductor said. "Merry Christmas, everyone!"

"Merry Christmas," various ones called out, their minds not on Christmas at that moment but the scene in the office.

As the conductor left, the stationmaster threw up his arms and let them fall to his sides.

"I don't know what to do," he said, his voice soft now. He looked at Ellen and shrugged. "I suppose it is all right. Since you are not well, it would be a pity to stop you here."

A great cheer went up in the room. "That's the spirit, Arnold!" "I knew you were a good man!"

Quickly the office emptied as the men hurried to board the train, many patting Ellen on the shoulder and back as they left.

"You better hurry," the stationmaster said to Ellen. "That train isn't going to wait for you."

"Thank you, sir," Ellen said warmly.

"You'll never know how deeply grateful I am."

Ellen was the center of much attention on the train. She didn't know how she managed to smile, laugh, and make conversation. She was empty now, so drained by the terror of the four days minus twelve hours, that she feared she might laugh at some harmless remark and, unable to stop, her laughter would tumble over and down into hysterical sobbing.

"You look a little pale," someone observed.

"I am somewhat weary."

"Well, we'll let you rest now."

"You're very thoughtful."

Ellen went almost immediately into a sound sleep and was startled when she heard a voice saying, "Wake up. Wake up."

"What is it?" she asked too loudly, afraid that the stationmaster had changed his mind and she was being ordered off the train.

"You have to get off, sir."

She looked into the conductor's face, panic threatening her sanity. "Is something wrong?"

"No, no," the conductor said. "We're at Havre de Grace. We have to ferry across the Susquehanna River. For the safety of the passengers, we ask them to ride on the ferry itself rather than remain in the coaches."

It was dark and cold when she stepped outside. A fine mist was falling, which chilled her quickly. She looked around for William, who always came to her whenever the train stopped. Ellen had never needed him as she did now, as the ferry moved into the cold, misty blackness of the river.

This wasn't like him. Where was he? She could make out the passengers in the light from the lanterns hanging along the ferry railing. He wasn't there! William was not there! He had been caught! She knew it!

She hurried around the ferry until she found the conductor. "Have you seen my servant, sir?"

The conductor chuckled. "Oh, he's probably run off and is in Philadelphia by now."

Ellen ignored his remark. "Could you find him for me?" she commanded.

The conductor was indignant. "I'm no slave hunter! If I had my way, every slave in the South would go free tomorrow. You'll get no help or sympathy from me!"

When the ferry stopped on the other side of the river, Ellen had not found William. She wondered if she should board the train or stay and see if she could learn what had happened to him.

She knew, however, that if he had been captured, his only solace would be knowing she was free. Reluctantly she got on the train. She was grateful for the darkness that hid the tears flowing down her face.

She didn't know that she had fallen asleep or how long she had been asleep when a voice awakened her. "Master?"

Her eyes opened quickly to see William bending over her. "Oh, William!" she exclaimed in a hushed whisper. "Where were you? I thought you — "

He put a finger to her lips to silence her, then smiled sheepishly. "I fell asleep. The conductor didn't bother to wake me when we came to the ferry. I woke up a few minutes ago and he told me that he'd told you I'd run away."

Tears flowed down her face again, but these were of relief. In the darkness she found his hand and squeezed it so tightly that he winced.

"It won't be long now," he told her.

When he returned to the Negro car, the conductor came in, chuckling. "Your master feel better now?"

"Yes, sir."

"Well, let me give you some advice, boy. When you get to Philadelphia, run away and leave that cripple and have your freedom."

"No, sir," William said indifferently. "I can't do that, sir."

"Why not?" the conductor wanted to know, surprised. "Don't you want to be free?"

"Massa good to nigger, sir. Massa good massa, him."

The conductor was outraged. "Well, of all the dumb things I've heard in my life," he said before storming out of the car.

William was sorry he could not tell the conductor the truth. He seemed like a good man, but one could never tell.

"That was good advice he gave you," William heard a voice say.

He looked around to see a black man seated across the aisle.

"Oh?" William said noncommittally, hiding his eagerness to talk to this well-dressed black, who by the erect way he sat showed that he had never lived a day in slavery. "I be better off with massa than free nigger any day," William said, hoping the man would take the bait.

The free black needed to hear no more to begin telling William about the black churches, fraternal organizations, businesses, and social life among the blacks of Philadelphia. "Why, there are blacks and whites eager to help someone like yourself escape from slavery." He told William the name and address of a white man who had helped many runaway slaves.

William listened intently, remembering everything he heard. When the man finished, his face eagerly awaiting William's response, William said, "Massa, he good massa to nigger. Me and massa grow up like brothers, me and massa did."

The free black got up in disgust. "You've got as much sense as a brick." He moved to the other end of the coach to be as far away from William as possible.

William regretted that the man would never know the truth, nor how helpful he had been. But they were too close to take any unnecessary risks.

William drifted off to sleep, repeating the

name and address of the white man over and over.

When the shrill whistle of the train awakened him, William opened his eyes and there, through the window, at the beginning of a day as gray as pewter, he saw the buildings of a large city. Philadelphia!

The train had scarcely slowed to a stop before he was out of the coach and hurrying to Ellen. Quickly they found a carriage and were being taken through the streets of the still city.

William put his arms around Ellen, and she began to cry. It was over, and she could cry now. Her body heaved with the force of the tears, as if the demons of fear and doubt were being torn from her body. She cried and William held her as if she were a child.

When the carriage stopped at the address, Ellen was so weak that William lifted her from the carriage. Through her tears she smiled, the green spectacles on her nose looking ridiculous now.

"Merry Christmas, husband," she said, feeling light in his arms, her arms around his neck.

Then she took the spectacles from her nose and tossed them high into the air. "Merry Christmas!" she shouted. "Merry Christmas, everybody!"

And she did not know her laughter from her crying, and the tears on her face shone like a smile.

Two

1

Almost two years had passed.

Was that a long time? Ellen wondered. On
evenings like this, when she sat in her rocking chair, gazing at the flames curling around
the logs in the fireplace, slavery seemed like
the smoke being drawn up the chimney.

Then she would glance at William in his
rocking chair, his head bowed almost prayer-
fully, reading a book. The sight of him slowly
deciphering the words was still so new that
the two years became a moment, and she
wanted to touch him to be sure that she was
not dreaming him, this house, and herself.
Especially herself.

"William?" she said softly.

"Hm?"

"Do you ever miss Macon?"

He didn't answer immediately, and it was
as if a great physical effort was required to
bring himself back from wherever the book
had taken him. But when he turned and
looked at her, he was smiling. "Only on nights
like tonight."

"What do you mean?" Ellen asked, concerned.

"Do you ever remember having to light a
fire on September the fifteenth in Macon?"

She laughed.

"I'll never get used to what they call weather here in Boston," he continued. "If there's as much snow this winter as there was last, I just might write Dr. Collins and tell him to come get me."

"Oh, William! If you can joke about it, you must be feeling like a free man."

"I always felt like a free man," he said, suddenly serious.

She knew that was true.

"Do you miss Macon?" he asked her after a long pause.

"Oh, I miss spring not coming in March," she answered quickly.

William chuckled. "It's May up here before the grass turns green. The slaves already got the cotton planted by then."

Ellen nodded. "And I can't get used to how much people hurry about up here."

There was another long pause before William asked gently, "Do you miss being a slave?"

She looked at him sharply, her cheeks flushing with — anger? embarrassment? hurt?

"That sounds awful, doesn't it?" she said finally, her voice barely a whisper. "How could somebody miss being a slave? But sometimes I feel like I'm not anything. I'm not what I was, but I don't know who I am. Does that make any sense, William? Please say it does."

He reached across the short space between their rocking chairs and took her hand.

"That's not the same as wanting to be a slave again. You know, there are some nights I sit here in this chair, reading, and suddenly I — I feel like everything is so new that I don't know what I'm doing or why. I read the most recent essays by Mr. Emerson and I read Mr. Garrison's *Liberator* newspaper, and there's so much I don't understand. Why, it takes me an hour to read what any school-child would read in ten minutes. But I don't confuse all those feelings with wanting to be in slavery again."

She squeezed his hand. "No, I guess I don't either. But it was simpler then."

After Ellen went to bed, William placed another log on the fire and pulled his rocking chair closer to its heat. The book lay closed on his lap.

Two years. He didn't know if Ellen should have recovered fully by now. How did one measure such? During the first months after their escape Ellen had scarcely been able to get out of bed for more than a day or two at a time. She cried for no apparent reason and couldn't stop. Gradually the episodes of crying lessened, and they moved to Boston.

Neither of them had anticipated the excitement the story of their escape elicited. They found themselves being asked to churches and antislavery meetings to tell their story. They met many of the famous people of the anti-slavery crusade, men like Wendell Phillips, Samuel May, the Reverend Theodore Parker, and women like Lydia Maria Child and Maria

Weston. He and Ellen were also famous now, he supposed.

Certainly their names had helped when he decided to open a store. He smiled to himself as he thought of the lettering on the window: "New and Second-Hand Furniture, 62 Federal Street, W. Craft, Prop." That was something! With Ellen doing seamstress work at home, they lived very well for two people who had been in slavery a mere two years before.

He had seldom thought about Macon since leaving. There was too much to learn, too many people whose friendships he wanted to cultivate. But Ellen was still suspicious of whites, though only he knew how uncomfortable she was eating at the same table with them when they were invited for dinner. After each dinner Ellen was silent for days afterward. It wasn't long before William began refusing the invitations, accepting only one for every five they received. Left to himself, he would've been out every night.

He knew that escaping slavery was not the same as becoming a free person. Sometimes he stopped by Lewis Hayden's clothing store and talked about things like that with him and the other fugitive slaves who congregated there.

"This freedom is like breathing new air," Lewis said once, pulling absentmindedly at the corners of his mustache. "I remember after me, my wife, and my baby escaped from slavery in Kentucky. Just the thought that I could do anything I wanted to, when I wanted to, and how I wanted to almost scared me to death at first. I could do anything I wanted!" He chuckled. "But first I had to know what I wanted to do. That's what freedom is. Knowing what you want to do."

William remembered sharing Lewis's words with Ellen, but she had acted as if she hadn't heard him. Something had happened to her during the four days of their escape, and he couldn't imagine what. He knew only that they had not had the child they had talked so much about while in slavery.

"Give her time," Lewis told him one afternoon when William sat crying in the back of Hayden's clothing store.

"But it has been almost two years!" William protested through his tears.

"And how much time is that when a person is trying to feel the shape of freedom?"

2

As befitted the owner of a clothing store, Lewis Hayden was always impeccably dressed. The smooth skin of his brown face appeared almost velvety surrounded by the neatly trimmed full beard and mustache. His light-brown eyes carried a pleasant expression, friendly but not so cordial that one would presume to slap him on the back in greeting or call him by his first name. That was an honor he extended to few. Though black and an escaped slave, Hayden had become as much a gentleman as any white Bostonian and moved quite comfortably in the parlors of those who considered their blue blood a birthright.

Lewis's birthright was to be the leader of the Boston black community. From his office in the back of his clothing store at 107 Cambridge Street in the West End, he listened to and helped solve the problems that were brought to him continually. Those with personal problems, or without jobs or places to live, eventually found their way to the man whose reputation for honesty was so great that his word was like a code of law.

Lewis kept an especially watchful eye on the six hundred fugitive slaves living in Boston. They were his kinspeople, and their problems were his. He understood what it was to suddenly, at the happiest of moments, begin crying. Was there a day when he did not think of his son, who had been sold away from him, that son he would never see or hear of again? The fugitive slave lived with a suffering that time could not ease, a pain that would never recede into memory.

That was why most fugitives passing through Boston eventually found their way to the back door of Lewis's store or to his house on Southac Street. He did not have to imagine their terror at being in a strange land and totally dependent on strangers. He did not have to imagine their loneliness in the face of a future so huge that it threatened to engulf and swallow them.

It was almost dusk on the evening of September 18, 1850, when he closed the store and settled at his desk to go over the account books. He had scarcely gone down one column of figures, however, before there was a soft knocking at the back door. He was not surprised. It seemed that whenever he had time to go over the accounts, a fugitive appeared, saying, "The Committee in New York sent me," or "Fred Douglass sent me."

But when he opened the door and peered out, he was surprised to see the short, stocky figure of Rev. Theodore Parker.

"Rev. Parker," Lewis said, opening the door and admitting the white man.

"Good evening, Mr. Hayden."

If Lewis was the leader of the black community, Theodore Parker was his equivalent among many antislavery whites. Outspoken and controversial, he was pastor of a church with seven thousand members. More important to Lewis was Parker's role as a leader of the Vigilance Committee, which patroled the streets constantly on the lookout for slave hunters.

"What brings you here at this hour?" Lewis asked, offering the minister a chair.

"Thank you," Parker responded, sitting down. He removed his hat to reveal a bald head that seemed too large for his body. "I presume then that you haven't heard."

"Heard what?"

"The news has come over the telegraph."

"No!" Lewis exclaimed. "No! I don't believe it!"

Parker nodded. "I'm afraid so. President
Fillmore has signed the Fugitive Slave Bill."

The Fugitive Slave Bill was one section of
the Compromise of 1850, making it a federal
crime to assist or hide a fugitive slave. Anyone caught doing so could be fined $1,000 and
sentenced to six months in jail. In addition
that person had to pay the slave's former
owner $1,000 for each slave he or she helped
escape.

Lewis slammed his fist on the desk. "We
are now officially a nation of slave owners!"

Parker smiled wryly. "Well, the President
has to enforce that law first." He patted his
coat pocket, where Lewis knew he carried his
pistol. "There'll be no fugitives taken out of
Boston. I promise you that."

"Well, we must increase our patrols immediately."

Parker nodded and stood to go. "I've already given the word. If the President wants
to declare war on freedom, I think we can
give him a fight he won't forget."

The next morning the chill clear air of approaching autumn was filled with the sounds
and smoke of exploding cannons. BOOM!
BOOM! BOOM! The city of Boston was cele-
brating the signing of the Fugitive Slave
Bill. BOOM! BOOM! BOOM! One hundred
times the cannons rattled the windows of
aristocratic homes on Beacon Hill, and the

greatness of America was toasted. One hundred times the cannons rattled the windows of the frame homes and rooming houses in the West End, where fugitive slaves were emptying bureau drawers and stuffing clothes into cardboard valises.

There was a small crowd waiting for Lewis when he opened his clothing store, and within an hour the store was so crowded one would have thought he was having the most spectacular sale of the decade. In an odd way that was true, but it was the men and women grasping at Lewis's arms who were suddenly for sale. They were mere things again that could be taken back into slavery on the word of any white person who knew or suspected. Now they were sorry that they had, perhaps in a moment of weakness, confided in the white person for whom they worked or with whom they were friendly. Could they trust that white person to keep silent now? The fugitives dared not think that there might be some fellow blacks whom they shouldn't have trusted.

"Keep your eyes open and your ears clean," Lewis repeated many times that day. "If you see any suspicious person, report it to a member of the Vigilance Committee. We will not allow anybody to be taken back into slavery."

They believed Lewis. He was in as much danger as they. However, some of the slaves were not so reassured by his words that they were willing to risk a knock on their doors in the middle of the night or being arrested as they walked to work one morning. They packed and wanted to be off to Canada as quickly as possible. Lewis knew that the cellars of his store and home were going to be full.

Members of the Vigilance Committee visited the fugitive slaves over the next several days, reassuring those who were willing to risk staying and helping those who wanted to leave. One evening when William returned home from his store, he found Ellen standing in front of the fireplace, jabbing at a log with the poker as if it were a half-live and dangerous animal.

"Ellen?" he said, concerned, going over to her.

"You tell your white friends to stay away from me!" she yelled, whirling around.

"What's wrong?" he asked. "What happened?" He reached out to touch her, but she moved away flinging the poker to the hearth.

"Some white lady from the Vigilance Committee was just here. What does she mean telling me not to be afraid?" Ellen affected a Boston accent and continued. " 'Mrs. Craft, you have many white friends in Boston who will lay down their lives for you and your husband.' " Ellen glared at William. "I'm so tired of your northern white friends telling me that they're my friends. What makes them think they can be my friends? Friendship is easy when you're born free and white. If she wants to be my friend, then when the slave hunters come for us, she can go to Macon in my place and I'll move into her big fine house."

"Nobody's going to take us back to Macon," William put in.

"No?" Ellen screamed. "And what makes you think that? Or have you forgotten that I was the one who didn't want us traveling all over Massachusetts telling the story of our escape? New Bedford, Northboro, Marlboro, Worcester, and a lot of other funny-named places. Churches were so filled that sometimes I was afraid somebody would push baby Jesus out of Mary's lap on the stained-glass windows so they could have a seat."

"Now, Ellen —"

"Don't you 'Now Ellen' me, William Craft! You enjoyed standing up there and being the big brave man for the white folks! They didn't come around afterward and stare at you like you were some freak. 'Why, you can't tell her from a white woman.' 'I don't believe she was ever a slave. How could a woman that white have been a slave?' You didn't hear them, William. Our friends! Well, give me my enemies! At least they know a nigger when they see one."

"Ellen!"

"Ellen!" she repeated sarcastically. "Ellen's name has been in every newspaper in the South by now, because Ellen couldn't convince her husband that we'd be beter off living anonymously. By now every white person in Macon knows where we are. If you don't

137

think that somebody is going to come up here looking for us, you're wrong! With this new law, there's nothing, absolutely nothing, that anybody can do to save us. Nothing!"

The scream that came from her body was like the shriek of a rare and gentle animal caught in a hunter's trap. William moved to take her in his arms, but she pushed him away and, sobbing, ran to the bedroom, slamming the door behind her.

3

Early on the afternoon of October 25, 1850, Ellis Loring, a lawyer and member of the Vigilance Committee, was seated in his office when a note was delivered to him.

> *Messrs. Charles Hughes and John Knight just left with warrants for the arrest of the Crafts.*

The note was unsigned, but Ellis knew it was from a young man whom the Vigilance Committee had strategically placed as a clerk to Judge Levi Woodbury.

Quickly Loring put on his coat and hat and took his carriage to Lewis Hayden's clothing store.

The Reverend Theodore Parker was returning from a trip to Plymouth that afternoon. As he approached the door of his home on Exeter Place, the door opened and his wife, Lydia, ran to meet him.

Before Parker could smile at this unaccustomed greeting, Lydia placed a folded note in his hand.

Committee meeting now.
LH

He folded the note and put it in his pocket. Then he looked at his wife and chuckled. "I should've known it was something like that. You've never run out to greet me."

She kissed him lightly. "And deny myself the pleasure of peeking between the curtains like some schoolgirl to watch you come up the walk? Never. Now, hurry!"

Ellen was finishing the seam on a gown when there was a knock at the door.

"Who could that be in the middle of the afternoon?" she muttered to herself.

The knock came again, more insistent this time.

"Just a minute," she called out, laying the dress carefully on the table. "Who's there?" she asked, cautious now as she approached the door.

"Rev. Parker," came the response.

Ellen opened the door. "What brings you here?" she wanted to know. "William is at the store."

"May I come in?" The minister smiled.

139

Ellen stood aside reluctantly and he walked in, removing his hat.

"I'm very busy now," Ellen said curtly.

"I apologize for disturbing you, Mrs. Craft, but my wife asked that I stop by for you. She has a dress that is in dire need of immediate repair and she claims that there is no one in Boston who can match the quality of your work."

Ellen allowed herself a stiff smile. "Well, why didn't she send the dress with you? I can't leave just like that."

Rev. Parker took her hand and looked at her seriously. "I'm afraid that there is no choice, Mrs. Craft."

Ellen caught the change in his tone, and she gasped. "You don't mean — "

"My carriage is waiting," Rev. Parker interrupted. "We must hurry."

The tears spilled from Ellen's eyes and rolled down her face.

"We don't have time to go to your house," Lewis told William as the two hurried through the alley.

"Won't take but a minute," William insisted. "You're sure Ellen's safe?"

"I told you. Rev. Parker took care of her personally. By now she is already at his house."

"Good. Good. I hear he keeps a loaded pistol on his desk."

Lewis chuckled. "Right next to a vase of flowers," he said, hurrying to keep up with

William as he turned down another alley. "Where're you going?"

"First thing I did after I rented the store was to find a back way from there to my house. Just in case. You understand."

Lewis understood. No one knew the back alleys of Boston like the fugitive slaves. They knew escape routes from any building they might be in.

"So Charlie Hughes and John Knight think I'm mighty important, huh?"

"Did you knew them?" Lewis asked.

"Know them! Charlie Hughes is one of the worst slave catchers in Georgia. And John Knight was the man my master hired me to when I was still a boy. He was the one almost caught us at the railroad station the morning we left Macon. I should've known he wouldn't rest satisfied."

They were approaching the back of William's house. They looked around, and seeing no one, William slipped quickly through a door in the fence. In a moment he had returned. "Let's go."

"I don't mean to pry, William, but what was so important?"

William opened his coat and Lewis saw the two pistols stuck in his belt.

"One is for Charlie Hughes and one is for John Knight. Now, where are they staying?"

"William! No! If you kill them, you'll hang for it."

"Some things are worth hanging for."

"Your wife, man! What about your wife?"

William stared at Lewis for a moment, then lowered his eyes. "What about my wife?" he said softly.

"You don't think it would make her happy to see you hang, do you?"

William shook his head. "I don't know, Lewis. I just don't know anymore."

"Well, I do," Lewis responded firmly, putting a hand on William's shoulder. "Let the Vigilance Committee take care of things."

After a moment William nodded reluctantly. "All right. But I'm telling you now. If Charlie Hughes and John Knight get within firing distance, they're dead men. You hear me?"

Lewis nodded. "You're my kind of man, William."

When they reached Lewis's home, William understood why he was Lewis's kind of man. Placed on tables throughout the house were loaded revolvers, and later, in the basement, William saw two kegs of gunpowder.

"If any slave hunter looks like he's going to take any slaves I'm hiding, I'll blow him and me to the highest star," Lewis explained.

William smiled and hugged Lewis to him. "You're my kind of man, Lewis."

4

The next morning black and white men could be seen carrying posters through the streets of Boston. Quickly these were nailed to fences, trees, and frame buildings. By the time the sun rose and the city began to busy itself for another day, all Boston knew that Charlie Hughes and John Knight were in town and what they looked like.

ATTENTION! ATTENTION!
Citizens of Boston
TWO SLAVE CATCHERS
CHARLIE HUGHES, average ht.,
165 pounds, black beard, blue eyes.
Scar on left cheek.
JOHN KNIGHT, tall, heavy,
sharp nose, brown eyes, brown hair,
fond of chewing tobacco.

When Hughes and Knight left their room at the United States Hotel at eight o'clock, a crowd of black men and women was waiting on the sidewalk.

"Go back to Georgia!" the crowd chanted as the two men stepped outside.

The two glanced nervously at each other, then started quickly down the street.

"Go back to Georgia! Go back to Georgia!" the crowd chanted, following them.

Hughes and Knight quickened their pace.

"Slave hunters! Slave hunters! Slave hunters!" the crowd yelled, changing the chant and hurrying to keep pace with the two white men.

So it was for Charlie Hughes and John Knight all that day.

It was late that evening when Theodore

Parker stopped his carriage in front of Lewis Hayden's house. His short, stocky body was hunched against the chilly wind. It was too cold for the end of October. Or maybe he was feeling the cold more now. He was only forty years old, but the winters were beginning to feel eternal and the summers all too brief. Some mornings he looked at himself in the mirror and saw a face that looked far older than its forty years.

He hadn't wanted any of this — the constant traveling across the country speaking against slavery, the late-night journeys to help fugitives on their way to Canada. He had planned to devote his life to study, and for many years he'd spent fifteen hours a day reading. He knew between twenty and thirty languages, he supposed, and had at least 16,000 books in his library at home. He chuckled to himself. Lydia maintained that the entire house had become a library.

He would've liked nothing more than to be sitting in front of the fire in his study, a book in his lap. But here he was, shivering, walking up the steps of a house in the West End, a pistol in his pocket. Why? he asked himself needlessly. All men — and women, as Lydia reminded him — were created equal in the eyes of God. He owed it to himself to try and look on things through God's eyes. It was that simple.

He did not have to knock on the door, knowing that on such a night Lewis would keep watch on the street from within the darkened house until sunrise.

The door opened and Parker stepped quickly inside. No words were spoken. It was a moment before Parker's eyes adjusted to the darkness and he saw Lewis standing by one window and William Craft by the other. Both men had pistols in their hands.

"Have our friends decided to leave the city?" Lewis asked.

"No. Though men with thinner skins would have," Parker responded. "We had people following them from the minute they stepped out of the hotel this morning until they went to bed tonight. Four men are watching the back and front entrances of the hotel through the night, in case they try to change hotels."

"Good," Hayden commented. "Maybe we'll have to make the crowds following them larger tomorrow."

"I don't think it'll make a difference to those two. The bigger the crowd, the more determined to stay they become."

"Then we'll simply be more determined."

"That may be a bigger task than we anticipated."

"What do you mean?" Lewis wanted to know.

"A message was delivered to me late this afternoon. That's the real purpose of my visit now." Parker turned and looked toward William. "Mr. Craft? A prominent citizen of Boston has an offer for you and Mrs. Craft.

If the two of you will allow yourselves to be arrested, then this gentleman guarantees that he will buy your freedom from your former owners, no matter the price."

"What!" William and Lewis exclaimed almost simultaneously.

"That's the message I was asked to deliver."

"I don't understand," William said slowly. "Why do we have to be arrested? If he's so concerned, why doesn't he just purchase our freedom outright?"

"That's precisely the point," Hayden responded heatedly. "If you and your wife are arrested first, then resistance to the Fugitive Slave Bill is broken. If you are bought off, the proslavery forces win."

"I think there is something I should add," Parker interrupted. "I spoke with Mrs. Craft this evening. She wants you to accept the offer."

"Oh, no!" Hayden exclaimed.

Parker could not see William's face and was glad. Whatever anguish was on his face should be seen only by the darkness.

"Did you tell her that this offer might be a trick?" William wanted to know.

"No. I didn't want to prejudice her, as I don't want to prejudice you."

No one spoke for some minutes. Lewis and Parker were not waiting to hear William's decision, because they were too alone suddenly with the burdens of their own lives and time, alone with the knowledge that whatever decision William made, it would be the right one and the wrong one. When the silence was broken finally, it was not William who spoke, but Lewis, his voice breaking on the darkness.

"When I was a boy, there was a white man who wanted to have his way with my mother. She resisted him and he went to my mother's master and said he wanted to buy her. Mother begged Master not to sell her to that man, but Master did. Mother refused to let the man have his way with her, so he put her in prison. The people in prison beat her and did everything they could think of to punish her. My mother began to lose her mind. She managed to get a knife once and tried to kill herself. A few months later she tried to hang herself. She was young and very beautiful. She was part Indian and had long straight black hair. It turned all white.

"The jailer became concerned and told her master that it might help her mind if she could see me. So she was brought to me, and when she saw me, she leaped at me and held me so tight I thought my arms were going to break. And she said, 'I'll fix *you* so they'll never get you!' And she grabbed at my throat to kill me."

He stopped and the silence rushed back in, heavy, as if it were about to burst from the weight of unshed tears and unheard sobs swelling in its womb.

Then there was a sardonic chuckle. "I

hadn't thought about this in years," Lewis continued. "One time a white man traded me for a pair of horses."

No one knew if minutes passed or hours. It didn't matter. Finally, when William spoke, he said only, "I have to see Ellen."

5

The next morning at breakfast Theodore told Ellen that they were going to try and bring William to see her that night. She left the table without a word and hurried through the book-lined hallway and up the three flights of book-lined stairs to her room at the top of the house.

Books, books, books. She'd never known there were so many books in the world. Books over the doorways, beside the fireplaces in every room, and in every room in the house. Mrs. Parker said she had refused to allow books in the dining room and kitchen. "If Theodore had his way, the food would be stored in sacks so he could use the shelves for books."

William would love this house, Ellen thought, gazing at the books lining the walls of her room. She went over to a shelf and took down a book. She opened it and turned the pages slowly. It was nothing but words on paper. Why would a man get excited by something like that? You couldn't hold words in your arms like you could a baby.

She stared at a page and spelled out a word

— t-h-e-o-l-o-g-y. But the letters did not become a word. They remained random letters of the alphabet, which was all she had managed to learn. She had watched William spelling out the letters to himself, and seen a wonderful smile break over his face when the separate letters coalesced into meaning. She would have given anything to have that smile.

It was different for her. William could open a book, or even speak, and enter a world that must be as beautiful as flowers opening in the spring. She remembered that first time she and William had attended an antislavery meeting and been introduced. When the crowd began shouting, "Speech! Speech! Speech!" she had been certain that William would smile shyly and shake his head. But he walked to the platform and spoke, the words coming one after the other as if he were reading a speech. She liked the words, the way they sounded together, the pictures they created in her mind, the feelings they brought forth from her heart. But she did not know the man from whose mouth the words came. And if that man was William, who was she?

In Macon she had known. She was Ellen, the slave and daughter of Ira Taylor. In Boston she was the runaway slave who looked like a white woman. Neither was much, but somehow who she was in Boston was worse. She was not a white woman, but neither was she what others thought a slave looked like.

Ellen remembered sitting at dinner parties

and knowing that white people did not know how to talk to her. If she were really white, they could talk to her about whatever white people talked about with each other. But she could tell they were thinking that she was not white. She was an ex-slave, a black woman. But how could anyone so white be black?

It had been dark for some time now. She sat in the parlor, and every time she heard a carriage approach, she was certain it was the one bringing William. When the steady, dull sound of the horse's hooves passed the house and faded until there was silence once more, she twisted the handkerchief in her hands a little more tightly.

Thus she was surprised when William walked calmly in.

"How —" she began, but could not continue. She looked into his tight, drawn face, noticing the lines of fatigue beneath his eyes. "Are you all right, William?"

"Fine," he said quietly, coming over to the divan where she sat. "You?"

"Fine. How did you get here? I didn't hear a carriage."

"I walked." He smiled.

"Walked?"

"From the nearby home of a Vigilance Committee member where I've been all day. We decided last night that they wouldn't expect me to go anywhere in the daytime, so I came early this afternoon. But it wasn't safe to come to this house until after dark. I came in through the cellar."

William sat down next to her. Ellen sat stiffly, glancing at him from the corners of her eyes nervously. It was a different kind of silence for them, and it didn't surround and entwine them like invisible colored ribbons. This was a hard silence, as thick as a mountain, and neither knew how to climb it and get to the other side.

"Would you like some tea?" Ellen asked finally. "It's rather chilly tonight."

"No thank you. I can't stay long. Rev. Parker and Lewis are extremely worried. They thought that Charlie Hughes and John Knight would have given up and gone back to Macon by now. They seem more determined to stay than ever."

"Then it would be better to let ourselves be arrested, have our freedom purchased, and have it all over with."

William placed his hand on top of hers. "Do you really believe that, Ellen? Do you really believe that somebody would buy our freedom after we were arrested?"

"What are you trying to say?"

"That it's a trick. If this man, whoever he is, wants to buy our freedom, then why doesn't he do it? We don't need to be arrested for him to buy our freedom."

"Well, perhaps there are reasons for that procedure that we don't know now," Ellen responded stubbornly, unable to refute William's argument.

"Even if he is telling the truth, we can't do it, Ellen. Can you imagine how demoralizing it would be for fugitive slaves all across the country if we allowed our freedom to be purchased for us? If we let our freedom be bought, we'll be saying that the Fugitive Slave Bill is just."

Ellen slid her hand from beneath William's. "I just want to be left in peace, William. I don't want all the fugitive slaves in America looking at us as their model. It's not fair! What about our lives? Don't our lives mean anything to you?"

Wililam reached for her hand again and held it tightly this time. "Maybe," he began quietly, "our lives don't belong just to us anymore. Maybe it isn't fair. We had no way of knowing that our escape would inspire so many. But that's how it is."

"Well, I don't like it! I feel less married to you now than I ever did in slavery."

"Then look into your own soul," he said gently. "I knew something was wrong. I thought maybe you hadn't recovered fully from the ordeal of our escape."

She laughed wryly. "I've been over that for quite some time. Whatever is wrong is between us."

He shook his head. "No, I don't believe so. Yes, I know I've changed some. I have a chance to live in the world as a man now, and not a thing. I like that."

"So you won't consent to letting this man buy our freedom," Ellen cut in coldly. "You won't consider that he might be telling the truth and that we wouldn't have to live in fear and hiding for the rest of our lives."

"I will not have my freedom purchased."

"Do you love freedom more than me?"

"I love freedom more than slavery," he said evenly.

"That wasn't what I asked."

"That's my answer. Can't you hear what I'm saying?" he asked, his voice acquiring a passionate urgency for the first time.

"Do you love this freedom more than you love me?" Ellen repeated angrily.

William released her hand and stood up. "Are you asking me to choose between freedom and you?"

He turned and walked toward the doorway. Then he stopped and stood for a moment before turning around and looking at her. "If you must have an answer, then, yes."

They stared across the room at each other for a moment, then he turned and started to walk through the door.

"William," she called softly.

He stopped but did not turn to face her. From the back he looked so ordinary, she thought. She'd always imagined heroes as tall and handsome, not short with big, thick hands.

Perhaps that was what she had not done. Loved freedom more than herself. To love the fear, the emptiness, and the utter terror of unknown and unknowable freedom, to love as Rev. Parker and William loved that letters

made words and words made visible the felt
unseen, just as a baby — that baby she would
have with William — was the unseen love of
a woman and a man becoming known.

She stood up and went to him. She had
only hated slavery. William had loved freedom.

"Very well, William Craft," she whispered,
putting her arms around him. "You trusted
me to bring you out of slavery. I suppose I
must trust you to bring me to freedom."

They hugged each other tightly, and then
he was gone.

6

Each morning the crowds outside the United
States Hotel were larger. Charlie Hughes and
John Knight were followed throughout the
day, fingers pointing at them, voices shouting,
"Slave catchers! There go the slave
catchers!"

Three times the Vigilance Committee had
the two men arrested on charges of conspir-
acy to kidnap and defamation of character
for calling William and Ellen slaves. Each
time bail had been set at $10,000 and some-
one, no one knew who, put it up.

Hughes and Knight refused to leave town,
however, not even after an angry black man
grabbed Charlie by the throat as he left the
hotel one morning. No one doubted that the
southerner would have been killed if the
crowd hadn't intervened.

154

Then word came that President Millard Fillmore was threatening to send seven hundred troops to Boston to capture William and Ellen. Theodore Parker and Lewis Hayden understood now why all their efforts to get the two slave catchers to leave town had failed. Clearly the President meant to enforce the Fugitive Slave Bill with military force. The Reverend Parker and Lewis were agreed: Hughes and Knight had to be forced out of town immediately.

On the morning of October 30 Theodore Parker led a group of sixty white men into the United States Hotel. They filled the lobby and hallway leading to Room 44.

When Hughes and Knight opened the door, Rev. Parker introduced himself politely, and then continued, saying, "I have come to request that you gentlemen leave Boston."

John Knight laughed harshly. "We'll leave when we get what we came for. And not before."

Rev. Parker smiled. "No, no. I'm afraid that you don't understand. You see, this is almost embarrassing, but I'm supposed to be a leader here in Boston, and I find myself at the point of being unable to control my people. Until now I've been able to restrain them. I take no pride in telling you, however, that they are at the point of ignoring my leadership. See for yourselves."

Knight and Hughes stepped into the hallway and were shaken to see it crammed with men, white men!

"I overheard one of them say that the only way you were coming out of your room today was dead," Parker continued. "Now, I'm sure that was just so much bravado. But then again, I'm not certain. I've never seen my people like this."

Knight and Hughes stepped back into the room, their faces drained of color. "We'll get in touch with the police," Hughes said. "They'll get your people and you out of here."

Parker shook his head. "Maybe I haven't been very clear. All I have to do is step into that hallway and tell those men that you aren't leaving town, and . . ." He threw up his hands and let them fall to his side.

Hughes and Knight went into a far corner of the room and whispered together for a few minutes.

"Is there a train out of here today?" Knight asked finally, his voice sullen.

"It leaves at two thirty," Theodore said solemnly.

"Very well. But I want you to understand that we'll be back, and when we do, we'll bring the United States Army with us."

Parker didn't respond except to say, "My followers and I will go with you to the train station to assure your safety."

7

Though Hughes and Knight had left Boston, it was apparent that William and Ellen were not safe there any longer. The President had not sent troops as he had threatened, but that did not mean that he wouldn't.

Ellen and William began disposing of most of their belongings. They couldn't carry much to England, the only place they were sure slave catchers couldn't reach them.

It was uncommonly warm the afternoon in the second week of November when William, Ellen, and Lewis Hayden gathered in Theodore Parker's study.

"Seems like we're having a touch of spring just for the two of you," Lewis said, smiling gently at them.

"I was thinking the same," Ellen said, her hand clasped tightly with William's.

"You look even more beautiful than the first time I saw you," William said, gazing at Ellen, whose long brown hair spilled over the shoulders of the white wedding dress.

"I'm glad you think so," she responded shyly.

"I know so," he said seriously.

Rev. Parker entered the study and smiled when he saw William and Ellen standing by the French doors leading to the backyard. "I don't think I've ever seen a more lovely bride and groom."

They turned and smiled.

"Do you remember our slave marriage, William?"

He chuckled. "It was a Saturday, and so hot I thought I was going to faint. We went out to Ira Taylor's plantation so your mother could see you get married. And old man

Taylor, who was as much of a preacher as a two-by-four, looked at you and said, 'Ellen, you want this man?' You said, 'I do.' He looked at me and said, 'William, you want this woman?' I said, 'I do.' Then he said, 'You can jump the broom, 'cause you married now.' And two slaves ran up with a broom. They held it about six inches off the ground and I took your hand and we jumped over the broom and that was it."

"That was just the way my marriage was," Lewis put in.

"Well, that kind of marriage wouldn't be recognized in England," Parker said. "And you deserve better," he added.

After the ceremony he reached into a drawer of his desk and took out a Bible. Placing it in William's right hand, he said, "You'll find all you need for you and your wife's souls in here." Then, reaching into another drawer, he took out a large bowie knife and, placing it in William's left hand, said, "Use it only if you have to, and not in hate. Now you may kiss the bride."

With the Bible in his right hand and the bowie knife in his left, William took Ellen in his arms and kissed her.

Then Ellen stepped back and looked at him. There was so much she wanted to say — that she was sorry for not having known it was not enough just to love him. Freedom had to be loved too.

But she didn't know how to say that for him to know, really know. So she took the

Bible and knife from his hands and put them on the desk. Then she took his hands and held them tightly in hers and looked deeply into his eyes.

And he knew.

Notes

"This Strange New Feeling" is a true story based on an account published in *The Anglo-African Magazine*, Vol. 1, No. 10 (New York: October 1859), pp. 321–4, reprinted in 1968 by Arno Press. The characters of Ras, Jakes Brown, and the slave owner are taken from that account.

"Where the Sun Lives" was suggested by the following entry found in Vol. 1 of Helen Catterall's *Judicial Case Concerning Slavery*, p. 210:

William Yates, a free man of colour, died in 1829, having first made his will, by which he gave his whole estate . . . to . . . in trust for his wife, Maria, who was his slave, to be paid over to her as soon as she could obtain her freedom, and get permission to remain in the

State. All the personal assets were insufficient to pay the testator's debts and Maria was sold.

"A Christmas Love Story" is a true story recounted in *Running a Thousand Miles for Freedom; or, The Escape of William and Ellen Craft from Slavery* by William Craft. William Craft's book, published in 1860, omits some details and incidents, which are recounted in Lawrence Lader's *The Bold Brahmins: New England's War Against Slavery (1831-1863)*, and John Daniels's *In Freedom's Birthplace: A Study of the Boston Negroes*. Additional information on the Crafts was found in William Lloyd Garrison's newspaper *The Liberator* for the years 1849 and 1850. All characters in my retelling of the story are historical. Lewis Hayden became the first black public-office holder in this country when, in 1859, he was appointed messenger to the Massachusetts Secretary of State. He held this position until his death in 1889. The Reverend Theodore Parker continued as a prominent figure in the antislavery struggle to the detriment of his health. He was eventually forced to go to Italy to try and regain his health, and died there in 1860 at the age of 49. A friend commented that he looked seventy. The characterization of Parker is based on the portrait in Lader's book. The story Lewis Hayden tells about his mother can be found in John Blassingame's *Slave Testimony*.

William and Ellen Craft lived in England from 1850 to 1868. Their two children were born there. It is believed that when they returned to the United States they went to Savannah, Georgia, to become heads of an agricultural school. The school was burned by the Ku Klux Klan in 1871 and rebuilt in 1873. William and Ellen returned to Boston in 1878. It is believed that William went to Africa at some period, but exactly when and for what purpose is not known. Likewise, I have been unable to trace William and Ellen after 1878.

Little is known of their two children, except that their son lived in England. Their daughter married W. D. Crum, who became the United States Minister to Liberia, where he died. Perhaps this was the occasion for William Craft's visit to Africa. A grandson, Henry K. Craft, graduated from Harvard in 1908 and taught at Tuskegee Institute, Alabama.

My own retelling of the extraordinary story of William and Ellen has its inception, perhaps, in 1961, when I moved from Nashville, Tennessee, to New York City. During my first summer in New York I met a young black woman with sandy brown hair, blue-green eyes, and an irrepressible spirit. One day I shared with her my feelings of elation at no longer living in the South, which at the time was still segregated. And while sharing these feelings, I said, for some reason, "I think I feel the way William and Ellen Craft felt."

She looked at me quizzically. "What do you know about them?"

I told her the story of their escape, though I don't recall now where or when I had first heard or read it. When I finished, I asked, "Why did you ask?"

She smiled. "Oh, William and Ellen Craft were my great-grandparents."

About the Author

JULIUS LESTER is the author of many highly acclaimed books including *To Be a Slave* (also available from Scholastic Point), which was a Newbery Honor Book in 1969, and *Long Journey Home*, a National Book Award finalist in 1972. His most recent book is *Do Lord Remember Me*.

Mr. Lester is a professor of Black Studies at the University of Massachusetts in Amherst, where he lives with his wife, three children, and stepdaughter.

Books chosen with you in mind from

point™

—Pass the word.

Living...loving...growing.
That's what **POINT** books are all about!
They're books you'll love reading and
will want to tell your friends about.

Don't miss these other exciting **Point** titles!

NEW POINT TITLES! $2.25 each